The tales they tell in storybooks
are always so sublime.
There's a happily ever after
for every once upon a time.
But fairy tales never do come true,
at least, not until I found you.

CINDERELLIS

AN MM ROMANCE FAIRY TALE RETELLING

Evie Drae

Once Upon a
Vegas Night

Published by

Published by
CLANDESDYNE
PO Box 621
Barberton, OH 44203-0521
www.clandesdyne.com

Cinderellis
Copyright © 2021 Evie Drae
Editors: Desi Chapman and Andrea Zimmerman, Blue Ink Editing, LLC

Cover Art
Copyright © 2021 Clandesdyne
www.clandesdyne.com

Paperback ISBN: 978-1-952695-05-6
Library of Congress Control Number: 2021903423
Paperback published February 2021
v. 1.0

For Kero and Thule. We love you and miss you, but your lights will shine brighter now that you're together again.

Chapter One

kaleidoscopic rainbow of colors danced around the darkness, creating enough light to set a lavish mood without detracting from the celebratory vibe. Ellis reinforced the effect with a careful combination of electronic dance music and remixed pop songs. His own personal list, one he'd cultivated over the past few years but rarely had the chance to use.

He ran a finger under the too-tight collar of his rented tuxedo and adjusted a few sliders on the mixing console to crossfade into the next song. It was a loud EDM club mix coming off the back of a softer pop track, which meant Ellis had to fine-tune a few more faders to normalize the audio. Tilting his uncovered ear toward the ceiling as he pressed the headphones over the opposite side, he nodded his satisfaction. It wasn't so loud people couldn't hold a conversation, but the beat pulsed under his skin and drew dancers to center stage.

The Colosseum at Caesars Palace Las Vegas had been Ellis's home away from home for over a decade. He'd worked as a stagehand for the iconic theater since he was fifteen, thanks to his stepfather, who served as the lead audio engineer. Filling the shoes of even a second assistant to Ray would be a dream come true, yet Ellis had never gotten further than unofficial mic wrangler.

Except for nights like this. Nights where manning the controls wasn't high on his stepfather's priority list and Ellis had a chance to shine. Even if Ray was the only one who knew it was really him running the show.

Growing up under the roof of the infamous Raymond Brunswick meant Ellis had more than enough informal training to operate the complicated equipment stretched out before him. He just didn't have the title to fit his experience. Yet. But the more times Ray handed over the reins, the more chances Ellis had to prove himself. Eventually the man would acknowledge his skill. He *had* to.

Even if there wasn't room for Ellis on the main sound team, he could still work toward that ultimate dream by taking on an official mic wrangler position. If Ray would approve the promotion.

The open-air sound booth, located at the heart of the rear orchestra, drew little attention from the raucous partygoers flooding the main stage. It was rare for the Colosseum to host such a shindig, especially one so small and exclusive. However, they'd signed a big-shot act for a limited six-month engagement, and celebrations were in order.

Ellis manipulated another crossfade to transition from the EDM track to an upbeat radio remix. The black-tie affair onstage continued to bop and sway to the beat, oblivious to the man controlling the flow of their movements. He grinned and leaned back in his chair. Someday, he'd do this for a living. He'd bring joy to countless people who'd never give him or the work he did a second thought.

That would be a hundred times better than his background rigging and carpentry jobs. At least running the audio would make him happy. Give him a reason to get up every day. Something more tangible than a dream.

Out of the corner of his eye, Ellis caught movement. He darted his head to the side with enough time to catch a figure, clad all in black, crawl under his console. Biting his lip, he pushed back his chair and peered into the dark space below. "Ah, excuse me—"

A flash of pale skin showed under an oversized hood. Full lips pursed into a silent *shh* as a slim finger tipped with black polish pressed against them. Ellis straightened and rolled his shoulders. He could leave the stowaway to their own business as long as they didn't bump anything or unplug any cords or...

Panic flaring in his gut, Ellis dipped his head a second time. "Look, I'm sorry, but there are a lot of important cords under there. It's not really a great place to—"

The figure crab-walked from beneath the table and flopped against the back wall of the sound booth, knocking the hood off as they did. The vibrant, multihued Ballyhoo lighting cut through the darkness with enough intensity Ellis could make out a rather grumpy-looking male scowling up at him.

Thick black eyeliner rimmed his eyes, their color indiscernible in the dim, infrequent illumination. His hair, somewhere in the brown spectrum, if the lighting could be trusted, stood out at odd angles. Whether purposeful or not, the effect was unnervingly sexy—like he'd just rolled out of bed after a proper romp. He drew his knees up and rested his folded arms on their bent surface, the scowl morphing into pinched exasperation.

"Anybody huffing down the aisle after me?"

Ellis cast his eyes over the empty front orchestra, then flicked them to the stage to assess the crowd before settling back on his mystery guest. "Doesn't look like anyone's headed this way."

"Thank fuck." The guy dropped his head against the wall. "Mind if I hang a bit? I need a breather."

3

"Ah, yeah, sure." As the current song ended, Ellis faded into the next before shoving the free side of his headphones farther off his ear. It was hard to hear anything but the music with the thumping track roaring into his covered left ear and the cavernous Colosseum mimicking the sound into his right. "If you're aiming to hide, you might have better luck in the corner. Less visibility if anyone does come looking."

The man's dark eyes danced in the variegated light before he nodded, slipped to the other side of Ellis's chair, and flashed a thumbs-up. "You're good people. Thanks, dude."

A few more songs came and went before Ellis shot another glance at his silent companion. He'd melted into the corner, leaning his head against the wall, his eyes closed, his hands resting on jean-clad thighs.

Hold the phone. Jeans? At a private black-tie party? Ellis peered closer, waiting for the fragmented light to tease over the guy again to reveal skinny dark-washed jeans, scuffed black-and-white Converse sneakers, and a plain black hoodie.

Okay, so he wasn't one of the event guests. Did that mean Ellis harbored an intruder? Unease settled in his stomach, churning acrid fluid up the back of his throat.

Ray would kill him if he fucked this up. No one was supposed to know it was a stagehand running the sound and not the high-paid lead audio engineer. If they came hunting for a party crasher gone rogue, Ellis would get caught.

He swallowed over the lump constricting his throat. Now wasn't the time to get spooked. He had to focus on getting his stowaway out of the booth before someone came looking for him.

Following the next song transition, Ellis slipped off his headphones and faced the man. Kohl-rimmed eyes blinked up at him, a crooked smirk tilting those full, irritatingly kissable lips.

Before Ellis could formulate a coherent sentence, the fugitive cocked his head and spoke. "You look ill, my man. You aren't gonna ralph, are you? If so, mind aiming it thataway?"

Ellis shook his head and straightened his back. His broad six-foot-three frame—honed by years of heavy-lifting duties—had a good six-plus inches and forty or so pounds on the guy huddled in the corner. Even if brute intimidation wasn't part of his usual repertoire, now was as good a time as any to use size to his advantage. He dropped his voice a few octaves and focused on hardening his features. "Who are you hiding from?"

The man laughed, wholly unbothered by Ellis's attempt at playing badass, and stretched his legs out to cross at the ankle. "Everyone. That lot's exhausting."

Shooting another glance at the party, Ellis ran his tongue over the tip of a canine. The energy pumping off the stage hadn't altered course despite the escapee's absence. Maybe no one knew he was there in the first place?

With a huff, Ellis slumped into his seat and dropped the tough-guy act. He'd never been good at it anyway. That kind of performance required personality traits he simply didn't possess.

The stowaway chuckled and ran a hand through his disheveled locks. "No one's gonna come looking for me here. Your space is safe. Promise. I told the tour manager, Kumiko, I was seeking quiet and refuge. She'll keep the wolves distracted for a bit."

Ellis frowned. If he knew the tour manager, he must be part of the new act. But why was he dressed like a bum at a fancy event in their honor? Maybe he was a roadie who hadn't been invited. Or, more likely, one of the band members who couldn't be bothered with following the rules because they so rarely applied to him. That made more sense. It would explain how he'd gotten away with a getup so far out of dress code. It would also explain why the tour manager would need to distract the other guests so he could slip away.

Great. Ray was adamant that Ellis didn't interact with the talent. Especially not when covering his stepdad's duties. What would this guy do if he saw Ellis hanging from the rigging later? Would he call Ellis out and get him in trouble?

Fuckin' hell.

"Are you part of Cinder's band?" Ellis played off the question as nonchalant, but nerves fired under his skin, drawing a shiver of unease in their wake.

"Am I part of...?" The man's brows crawled up his forehead. "You don't know who I am?"

Ellis shrugged and reached for his headphones, repositioning them over his left ear so he could work the next fade. When the techno beat rolled through the speakers, a squeal erupted from the stage. He ignored it in favor of squinting an eye at his guest. "I know music and voices, not faces or names."

"Huh." The corner of the man's mouth pinched in, and he nodded. "Makes sense."

When nothing more was said, Ellis sucked in his bottom lip to hide his frustration. He needed to know how deep he'd landed in this shit pile. Which meant getting an answer to his question. "So you're a member of the band, then?"

"Oh." The guy licked his lips and gave a little sniff. "Yeah, I am."

Ellis deflated at the confirmation. It meant he'd spend the next six months hiding in the rafters or behind set construction rather than working the mic check duties Ray had only recently bestowed on him. His first step in the right direction after a decade of dashed hopes and this man had ruined it without even trying. Without even *meaning* to.

Biting back a sigh, Ellis returned his focus to the mixing console. He adjusted a fader for the sole purpose of busying his hands, not because the sound was unbalanced.

Why didn't life have a slider bar he could tweak and fine-tune to fade from one scene to the next as easily as he transitioned between songs now? Finding equilibrium in the real world was a hell of a lot harder than it was in a sound booth, that's for sure. But the chaos and abnormalities that happened in between the moments of balance were what made life interesting. Who wanted to race through their existence, anyway?

When the time was right, he'd get his chance. A *real* chance. One where he could prove his worth and earn a permanent spot by his stepfather's side as an assistant to one of the greats. Then someday, when Ray retired, maybe Ellis could take Ray's place. Maybe *he* could be the sound god worshiped for his astute knowledge and expert skills.

Better yet? Maybe he could make Ray proud. And when his stepdad turned that gleaming, delighted smile on *him* for a change, all his struggles would be worth it.

Chapter Two

Cinder couldn't fight the grin tugging at his lips. When was the last time he'd come across someone who didn't know who he was?

As the son of Julia and Clyde Cinderford, two legends of the music industry who still performed to sold-out crowds to this day, he'd spent his childhood on the road. His parents owned lavish houses in three different cities across the globe but never stayed in any of them for longer than a month or two at a time. Long enough to record a new album and they'd be off again.

When he was fourteen, Cinder landed a career of his own, guaranteeing a future comprised of the same chaotic schedule he'd lived as a child. Something he didn't regret. Not really. He loved everything about his life, including all the chaos that went with it.

But this was what he'd hoped to find during his furlough from the tour circuit. *Normalcy*. A sense of being part of something human and routine. Something he hoped would ground him in a way he'd never had before.

With six whole months stretching before him at a single location, all while staying in the gorgeous desert abode he'd purchased for the occasion, Cinder planned to discover what it meant to be *home*. A foreign concept, to say the least, but that was something he aimed to change.

And what better way to start than by finding someone who didn't know—or seem to care—who he was?

The audio engineer frowned when Cinder admitted to being part of the band, as if the news somehow displeased him. That wasn't a reaction he was used to, but it was certainly intriguing. What would he think if he knew Cinder wasn't part of the backup band—a group that morphed and changed depending on his tour schedule—but the lead singer himself?

Delighted laughter rose from the stage when the sound dude fiddled with the glowing control panel again and the music shifted tempo.

There was no question, this guy was good at what he did. Cinder's lead audio engineer on the tour—Lizbeth, an often-irritable pixie of a woman—considered playlist management glorified disc jockeying and far beneath her. But it took skill to keep a discerning group like the one Cinder traveled with happy. Plus, his fades were gorgeous and perfectly timed. "So have you been running the audio here a long time, Mr....?"

The man snapped his gaze to Cinder, his frown deepening into an adorable pout. He shook his head and redirected his attention to the multicolored monstrosity of backlit buttons and gadgets.

Despite growing up around all the technical equipment necessary to run a stage production, Cinder avoided the stuff. It wasn't his forte, and he had no qualms admitting it. The tech folks were usually grateful for that fact.

Overinvolvement from front stage divas was a frequent cause for job relocation in the music biz, and Cinder tried his damnedest not to be one of those overbearing assholes his crew ranted about. He valued his team. Without them, he couldn't do what he did.

Which meant making nice with his new audio engineer should be top priority. Yet something kept him from going the full disclosure route right off the bat. Was there anything wrong with developing a relationship not based around his fame? Just this once? Just for a little while?

"So..." Cinder gave a wave in the sound guy's peripheral vision, grinning when a pair of light eyes shifted to meet his own. "That trail off there was an attempt at getting your name. I'm a tad elevated on the social awkwardness scale, so how about I try that again?" He held out a hand, suppressing a chuckle when the guy scrunched his nose at the offer. Not the typical reaction, but he loved it. "Name's Henry. What's yours?"

It wasn't a lie, even though it felt a bit skeevy. Cinder hadn't adopted the shortened version of his last name in place of his given one until he embarked on his own career as a teen. Because, seriously, Henry was *so* not the moniker of a rock star. The fact his rocker parents had bestowed such a travesty on him was downright criminal.

Still, if he dropped the Cinder bomb, this conversation would be over, and he wasn't ready to give up a shot at something so pleasantly ordinary.

Taking Cinder's outstretched hand with his large, calloused palm, the man tilted his head and studied Cinder a beat. "Ellis."

Nibbling the tip of his tongue, Cinder rolled the name around his mind—strong, sturdy, and sexy, like its broad-shouldered owner. "I dig it. So, Ellis, how long have you been an audio guru?"

Ellis speared a hand into his styled-back blond hair and caught it on his earphones, sending them clattering to the floor. He cursed under his breath as he fumbled around the darkened space. Once again, he didn't answer Cinder's question.

Curious. Was it a purposeful refusal or did he not like to talk? Maybe chatting put him off his game. Lizbeth turned into a raging beast if anyone interrupted her while she was "plugged in." He should consider himself lucky Ellis wasn't biting his head off.

Ellis was kind enough to provide sanctuary from the suffocating mob onstage. The least Cinder could do was keep his trap shut.

He caught sight of the dropped headset when a bright, purple-white flash cut through the booth. It had fallen under Ellis's chair. Leaning forward, Cinder blindly felt for the earphones, startling when another swoop of light—blue segueing into a pulse of green—illuminated the space. He and Ellis were nose to nose.

Ellis drew back but not before Cinder got his first good look at his face.

Hot damn. Were all Vegas men that strikingly gorgeous, or was Ellis an anomaly? Cinder couldn't decipher the true shade of Ellis's eyes, but they were pale. Hauntingly, beautifully pale. His features could've been sculpted from a block of marble, they were so solid and angled. And that jaw—*holy hell*—paired with a set of soft, plump lips sent Cinder's brain immediately south, imagining that mouth and that strong, squared-off jaw doing something inappropriate and wonderful.

Squirming at the ache between his legs spurred on by his lewd imagination, Cinder snatched the earphones and thrust them into Ellis's lax grip.

Ellis juggled the headset a few times before firming his hold. He mumbled a thank-you, slipped them over one ear, and returned to his work without sparing Cinder another glance.

Satisfied to simply be free of the social niceties and overwhelming press of the crowd, Cinder settled into the dark corner and kept his unspoken promise. He didn't say another word.

When a hand landed on his shoulder sometime later, Cinder jerked awake. He had no clue how long he'd been asleep, but based on the near-silence and absence of festive Ballyhoo lighting, he could guess it had been a while.

Ellis stood over him, looking rumpled and sexy. The top two buttons of his dress shirt were popped open, his bowtie undone and hanging loose beneath the crisp collar. He no longer wore his headphones, and in the bright glare of the house lights, platinum streaks were visible weaving through the golden honey of his beach-boy blond locks. It was an enviable color, and the waves looked thick and soft. Cinder itched to run his fingers through them.

Suppressing a yawn, he shoved to his knees and peered around Ellis to be sure the party had dispersed. Thank heavens it had. "I slept through all the fun, huh? What an epic bummer."

"It's after three. Everyone cleared out for an after-party about forty-five minutes ago." Ellis ran a hand over the back of his neck, casting his eyes to the floor. "I figured you'd want to wait until the coast was clear, so I let you sleep a while longer. Hope that's okay."

"*Shit.*" Cinder jumped to his feet, all trace of sarcasm gone from his voice. He scrubbed both hands over his face in a vain attempt at increasing the blood flow to his tired brain. "I'm sorry, dude. The last leg of the tour was brutal. Different city every night. I guess I was more wrecked than I realized."

Ellis's cheeks pinked. "'S all good. You weren't bothering me."

When Ellis scraped his teeth over that plump bottom lip, the ache returned to Cinder's traitorous groin. He shoved his hands into the pockets of his hoodie and forced it down to hide the growing proof of his inexplicable attraction to the man towering over him.

He'd never been attracted to a particular sex or gender, but more a *type*. It didn't matter to him how someone identified or what body parts they were working with below the belt. It was who they *were*—their essence, as he liked to call it—that caught his attention.

But big and bulky wasn't his usual style. He leaned more toward submissive personalities, and people Ellis's size who possessed those tendencies were a rare breed. At least, in Cinder's experience. Although his wasn't exactly typical. Nothing about his life, nor his sexual adventures, followed the status quo.

Still, something about Ellis's shy, quiet nature lured him in. Or maybe it was his unfathomable beauty, so unexpected when paired with his husky build. Either way, Cinder didn't want this to be the last they spoke.

Once things got rolling on the show and routine settled in, he might not have a viable excuse to seek out the audio engineer. Any reason he could come up with would be something Kumiko or someone else on his payroll could handle. Which meant, if he wanted to see Ellis again, he needed to act now.

"So you got any plans for tonight?"

Ellis's brows bounced in a flash of surprise. "What, you mean now?"

"Yeah, after you close up shop." Cinder licked his lips and ignored the voice at the back of his mind telling him he sounded like a dumbass. Of course Ellis had plans. Plans to go home and sleep. It was after three in the morning, after all, and he hadn't recently woken from a long, refreshing nap. "You're a Vegas man, and this is the real city that never sleeps. Thought maybe you had something fun on the schedule."

"If you consider falling face-first into my bed fun, then sure, I've got plans." The corner of Ellis's mouth tugged into a half smile, and that sight alone nearly undid Cinder.

He couldn't fathom what a full-wattage grin would do if that half-assed little thing sent his belly churning.

What was his deal? Since when did he lust after someone who hadn't shown an ounce of interest in return? It wasn't his style to pursue lovers. All he had to do was sit back and wait for the right one to come after him, have a little fun, and move on to the next city and the next warm body vying to share his bed.

But this was different. Ellis was different. He didn't give a rat's ass who Cinder was, which meant the small smile he'd offered was genuine and meant for *Henry*, not the gilded trappings that accompanied his public persona.

"Fair enough." Cinder licked his lips. "What about tomorrow? It's our last night of freedom before the show begins. I'd love to play tourist for an evening with someone who actually knows their way around the city."

Ellis rubbed a hand over the back of his neck and squinted an eye. "Ah, there's a lot that still needs done around here to get ready. I really can't. I'm sorry."

"Sure, yeah. Of course." Cinder hid his disappointment with a wide grin. "How about a rain check?"

Pressing his lips together, Ellis nodded. "Yeah, okay."

If tonight wasn't meant to be, so be it. Cinder would be around for the next six months. Neither of them would be going anywhere.

Chapter Three

Ellis propped the push broom in its designated corner of the janitor's closet and gave the pull-chain a tug, casting the small room into darkness. He backed out, closed the door, and jiggled the handle to be sure it was locked.

When he turned around, a startled yelp escaped his throat.

"Whoa, sorry, dude." Henry held up both hands, palms out, and grinned. "Wasn't trying to sneak up on you, but I caught your beachy blond mop out of the corner of my eye. Had to come say hey, long time no see. Where've you been hiding?"

Nerves coiled in Ellis's belly as he cast his gaze over Henry's shoulder to be sure no one else was around. "Nowhere. Been busy, that's all."

That wasn't a lie. He was always busy, and he wasn't hiding—not by choice, at least.

As expected, after confessing to Ray about his run-in with Henry, Ellis had been taken off all sound-related duties. His stepfather had also spoken with the head rigger and gotten Ellis switched to the fly gallery, which assured he was out of sight on a catwalk above the stage during performances and rehearsals.

Henry pursed his lips and nodded. "Sure, yeah, it's been a hectic few weeks, what with trying to get all the kinks worked out of the show and all. Haven't seen you around, though. Even had the tour's sound goddess, Lizbeth, ask after you. Got some serious grumpy 'tude from the lead audio douche in return. What's that guy's deal, anyway? He's a real sour ass."

Heat pricked at Ellis's cheeks. He ducked his head and offered a noncommittal shrug. Talking ill of his stepfather was out of the question. That was a surefire way to lose his job. Among other things. "Ray's the best of the best. You guys couldn't ask for a better person to run your audio."

"I dunno, Lizbeth isn't impressed, and in my humble opinion, she's the industry standard for awesome." Henry shoved his hands into the pockets of a casual pair of jeans. His whole appearance had shifted from the grungy-roadie look to a country-boy vibe. Gone was the unnaturally pale skin and artfully chaotic hair, replaced instead by an array of freckles and soft, shaggy waves that fell into his eyes. "What about you? Why aren't you out there running mic checks and generally being your baller sound geek self? I bet you're a thousand times better than that old dick bag."

Something between an anxious laugh and a hiccup fell from Ellis's lips. He cringed. Did he go with honesty or scrabble for a lie? Considering lying had never been his strong suit, Ellis sighed and shifted his stare to meet Henry's.

His pulse quickened when gorgeous hazel irises blinked at him beneath thick lashes. Even without the dramatic eyeliner he'd sported at their first meeting, that natural dark fringe made Henry's eyes pop. It was all Ellis could do to keep his mouth closed and his expression neutral.

Henry's beauty nearly stole his breath away.

"I'm not on the sound team. I was covering that night, but I'd, ah, really appreciate if you kept that to yourself." Ellis squinted an eye. "It could kinda get me in trouble if anyone found out."

Henry frowned. "Dude, how are you not an audio guy? You were rockin' those faders, and everyone had a blast with your tune selection."

Ellis shrugged and fought back a grin. How many times had he yearned to hear someone say something like that to him? And for it to be Henry? Something about that made the compliment even more special. "I was just running a playlist."

"Yeah, whose playlist?" Henry lifted a brow. "Yours?"

"It doesn't matter." Ellis shifted his feet. He needed a change of subject before Henry dug too deep or asked questions he'd rather not answer. Making any further connection between him and Ray could only lead to trouble. "What're you doing here, anyway? There's no show tonight, and I didn't see a rehearsal on the call board."

On the nights the Colosseum went dark, Ellis worked his second job as the off-shift caretaker. It was his responsibility to handle any maintenance duties or cleaning needs not taken care of during open hours. In return, he was given some storage space and a cot in the old green room, which had been made obsolete after the remodel. It wasn't fancy, but it saved on travel time and gave him a space to call his own.

In a town as expensive and traffic heavy as Vegas, those were perks well worth the extra work.

"I could ask you the same thing, you know." Henry cocked his head and smirked. "I was bored at home and forgot my guitar here. Thought I'd pop by and grab the ol' girl so we could entertain each other, but I found something even better. Human company."

When Henry waggled his brows, realization sent Ellis's stomach churning as unease battled with an achy longing. He'd been tasked with staying as far away from the talent as possible. Especially Henry. But the thought of spending a carefree evening in Henry's company sounded almost too good to be true. He couldn't remember the last time anyone other than his stepfather had sought his companionship, and Ray only ever wanted Ellis around as a means to an end—someone to do his bidding so he could put his feet up and get sloshed.

Still, as much as he wanted to steal an evening for himself and get to know Henry better, it would be safer if he kept his distance.

"Ah, sorry, but I was actually headed home." Again, not a lie. He'd been on the way to his cot for a much-needed early turn-in. It wasn't too often he had the chance for a full night of sleep, and it made for the perfect excuse. "Why don't you call one of your bandmates? I'm sure they're out partying somewhere and would welcome you along."

"Meh, I don't really hang with those dudes." Henry scrunched his nose, further highlighting those adorable freckles his stage makeup had kept hidden. "I think fate's trying to tell us it's time to cash in that rain check you promised me. Why else would we both be here at the same time on our day off?"

Because Ellis wasn't off, that's why. In fact, he hadn't had a full day to himself in recent memory. He ran his tongue over the back of his teeth as he chewed on Henry's words. He *had* promised a rain check to escape the last invitation. How many times could he get away with running from Henry before Henry caught on and demanded to know why Ellis was so damn scared to be friends?

"Okay, but I can't stay out too late." When Henry cracked a delectable grin and pumped a fist in the air, Ellis couldn't help but return the smile. It was damn near infectious. "Did you have something specific in mind?"

"Yes." Henry spread his arms. "Anywhere that isn't here. I've lived in Vegas for a month now and haven't seen anything but the Colosseum and my house. I need some fresh scenery before I start to mold."

Ellis chuckled. "That doesn't narrow things down much. Were you thinking of getting dinner? Drinks? Seeing a show?"

Henry pursed his lips and squinted his eyes. "Food is a must, and drinks fall high on the list. You're from around here, right?"

That was an understatement. Ellis hadn't left Clark County more than a handful of times his whole life, each of those trips only a couple of miles outside the county limits at most. "Born and raised."

"Excellent. Take me somewhere nontouristy. The more hole-in-the-wall, the better."

Hell. Ellis hadn't spent much time out and about, especially as an adult. If Henry wanted a tourist-trap recommendation, Ellis could've prattled one off easily enough. Living in the city meant learning its offerings, more as a rite of passage than because he frequented the establishments. But nontouristy? He had nothing to offer in that department.

How would that look to Henry? He'd admitted to being a native Las Vegas resident, yet he couldn't provide a single suggestion not printed in a sightseeing pamphlet.

Ellis patted his back pocket and sighed. His wallet was on the stack of boxes he used as a nightstand. "Can you give me a minute? I have to grab something."

"Sure, no prob. I'll come with you." Henry closed the distance between them and cocked an expectant brow. "You know, you never did say why you were here."

Biting back a groan, Ellis headed for the old green room. He didn't want Henry to see his living space, but it would be easier to let him follow and hold him at the door than to argue against the idea of him joining in the first place.

He wasn't too keen on the notion of telling Henry his real job, but lying was out of the question. They had at least a few hours of close proximity and conversation ahead of them. No way Ellis could keep a runaway lie secret for that long, but nothing said he couldn't be vague. Maybe Henry wouldn't be interested enough to question him further. "I work here."

"Well, no shit, Sherlock." Henry chuckled and gave Ellis's shoulder a playful shove. "But the show's dark tonight. Why are you here?"

So much for a lack of interest. Ellis swallowed and angled a glance at Henry. "I have two jobs here. I only work the second one on days there's no show."

"Hold up, don't you get *any* days off?" When Ellis shrugged, Henry narrowed his gaze. "What is it you do, if you aren't in audio?"

Ellis rubbed at the back of his neck and averted his eyes. He wasn't ashamed of the work he did. They were good, honest jobs, and he enjoyed them. Especially when his stepdad let him help with the sound. But Henry might look at Ellis differently knowing he'd not only falsely led him to believe he was an audio engineer, but his real position was a low-level grunt worker. And a glorified janitor. "I'm a stagehand. A rigger, to be exact. On the show's off days, I'm the caretaker."

He used their arrival at the old green room to prevent Henry from responding. He didn't want the rich musician's pity any more than he wanted his disgust. No matter where Henry was on that spectrum of emotion, he could keep his thoughts to himself if Ellis shifted the focus of their conversation. "Give me a sec. I have to grab my wallet, then we can head out."

But rather than slipping into the room unaccompanied as he'd hoped, Ellis found Henry following so close on his heels it was impossible to close the door behind him.

Henry stopped short at the sight of Ellis's cot. He moved his stubbled jaw back and forth. "Dude, do you live here?"

With a huff, Ellis dropped his shoulders. Mortified heat prickled at his cheeks. "It makes things easier. I work a lot of hours, so having a place close by that doesn't require me to fight all that crazy traffic on the Strip saves a lot of time."

He'd lived with Ray for most of his life. After his mom passed away when he was nine, his stepdad and younger stepsister were all he had. Thankfully, Ray begrudgingly agreed to remain his guardian rather than dumping him in the system. But when Ellis bumped up to full-time rigger after high school, they couldn't share rides anymore. Ray often went home for the day when Ellis still had hours of work left. Plus, he was due in way earlier.

About five years ago, when Ellis was twenty-one, Ray told him to find a place of his own. He was tired of Ellis stumbling into the house late at night and waking him up early in the morning. Thankfully, the caretaker position opened not long after that, and since management already knew Ellis, they agreed to his request to bunk down in the old green room in lieu of payment.

In the end, it proved to be a major upgrade. The sleeping arrangements were comfortable, he had free use of the showers when the talent went home for the night, and it saved him from the hours he'd spent traversing the miserable public transportation system to get to and from his childhood home in Boulder City.

Ellis grabbed his wallet off the nightstand box and glanced at his frowning companion. *Dammit.* Not only did he face the challenge of finding a nontouristy spot that wouldn't gross Henry out, he'd also have to endure more conversation about a topic he'd prefer not to discuss. But the scowl on Henry's mug clearly read *this chat isn't over.*

Fuckin' hell.

Chapter Four

While McMullan's Irish Pub off Tropicana was far closer to the Strip than Cinder had intended, its dimly lit atmosphere and raucous patrons provided the perfect blanket of anonymity. Especially when they scored an empty table at the back.

Despite the robust menu, they both landed on fish and chips with a pint of Guinness. When the flirty server, either a true-blooded Irish woman or an actress with enviable skill, bounced off to place their order, Cinder leaned back in his chair. He pulled the faded and worn brim of his favorite baseball cap down to better hide his obnoxious eyes—his most recognizable feature when he wasn't wearing his stage garb—and tilted his chin toward Ellis. "So whataya say we shake all this polite crap and have a real conversation?"

Despite the short distance, it had taken them fifteen minutes to get from Caesars to McMullan's by cab. The entire way, Cinder tried prying an exchange from Ellis that went beyond the required social niceties, but his efforts had fallen flat.

Man of a thousand words, Ellis was not.

As if to prove the validity of that statement, Ellis shrugged and fidgeted with the silverware roll instead of making eye contact or supplying a verbal response to Cinder's request.

Chuckling, Cinder sat forward again, resting his elbows on the table. "Come on, man, throw me a bone, will ya? I'm starved for human interaction that doesn't revolve around some aspect of who I am onstage."

The raw truth behind those last words belied Cinder's attempt at lighthearted humor, but he kept his patented grin in place when Ellis cast a glance his direction.

"I'm not really much of a talker."

No shit. Cinder sucked in his bottom lip to stop the snarky retort from popping free. He couldn't blame Ellis for his reticence. Not everyone was as loudmouthed as Cinder. Plus, there was a clear demarcation in Ellis's demeanor following Cinder's careless interrogation back at the theater.

It wasn't his place to ask such personal questions of a man he didn't even know. Even less so when those questions came with shocked judgment written all over them. It was no wonder Ellis had clammed up after Cinder expressed surprise over his work and living arrangements.

Cinder sometimes forgot the silver spoon lodged up his ass wasn't a cursed blessing shared by the world. He couldn't afford to forget that with Ellis. Not if he wanted this friendship—or whatever it might become—to work. And he did. He so, so did.

Resolved to act as human as possible so as not to scare Ellis away, Cinder cleared his throat and tapped his fingers to the beat of a familiar pop song playing over the steady din of the bar patrons. The group had opened for him on his last domestic summer tour. They had some impressive raw talent. No doubt they'd go far.

The server dropped off their beers then, offering a prolonged view of her ample breasts as she bent over, the luscious mounds barely contained within a cherry-red tube top perfectly matched to the slash of vivid color adorning the pout of her lips. The shirt was so undersized it rode up her midriff while still managing to leave her cleavage spilling over the neckline. The scant scrap of fabric masquerading as a skirt did little to make up for the lack of material up top.

Rather than attracting either man's attention as she had so undoubtedly hoped, Cinder found his gaze drawn to Ellis, who happened to angle his own Cinder's way at the exact same time. They both grinned, as if exchanging some unknown inside joke, and the server huffed in defeat. She checked to make sure they had everything they needed, let them know their food would be out shortly, then disappeared into the crowd.

"So." Cinder tried another smile and suppressed a sigh of relief when Ellis offered one in return, even going so far as to make eye contact again. "How long have you been working at the Colosseum?"

Ellis took a sip of the dark liquid courage and squared his shoulders, as if preparing for battle. "I started there as a part-time stagehand when I was fifteen. Been there ever since."

Cinder collected a trickle of overflow on his knuckle as he ran it up the side of his pint glass. When he brought the drop of bittersweet beer to his lips and licked his finger clean, Ellis's brows twitched ever so slightly, and he downed another gulp of Guinness.

That made sign number two in as many minutes. Could it be Cinder's hopes of finding something beyond a simple friendship with Ellis might be less of a stretch than he'd first presumed?

Bolstered by the thought, Cinder took a long swallow of his own beverage to hide his grin. "You must really love the work to stay there so long."

"I do. Some great acts have come and gone over the

past decade or so, and I'll always be able to say I was a part of them, in some small way. Including Cinder's." Blessedly, Ellis had returned to fidgeting with the silverware roll, so he didn't see Cinder tense at his own name. "That guy has the voice of an angel, I swear. It must be something else being on the stage with him, huh?" Then, almost under his breath, he mumbled, "I'd love to mix for him someday."

When Ellis raised his gaze and caught Cinder's, a dreamy smile pulling at one corner of his lips, Cinder's throat closed. If it weren't for the purity and substance behind Ellis's words, Cinder might assume he knew the truth and was needling at Cinder for a reaction.

But no, he'd simply been offering the most genuine compliment Cinder ever received. Because he didn't think the artist himself was present.

Fuck.

He couldn't do this. He couldn't lie to Ellis, even if it wasn't so much a *lie* as an omission. Still, in that moment, only one question would pass his lips. "Why don't you? You're brilliant behind that console. I saw the proof with my own two eyes. And ears."

Confusion morphed into pain before Ellis's gaze fell to his lap. "It's complicated."

After encountering the jackass lead audio engineer, Cinder could guess where the "complicated" came in. But before he could offer an opinion on the subject, their meals arrived. The server was less overtly flirty this time around, but she still lingered longer than necessary, and by the time she'd disappeared back into the crowd, the moment was lost.

As was Cinder's chance to come clean.

The conversation drifted to lighter topics. Simpler topics. Aimless chatter Cinder rarely had the chance to enjoy with anyone other than Kumiko and Lizbeth, his two rocks on the road crew. A married couple who graciously took him on as a third wheel when his battery inevitably drained to empty and he needed real human contact to re-charge.

They split the bill for dinner, as they had the cab fare. When they stepped out of the cool interior of the bar and into the stagnant heat of a summer evening in the des-ert—still too early to have cooled off, but without the op-pressive sun to further warm their skin—Cinder suggested they walk back to Caesars.

To his delight, Ellis agreed, and their idle conversa-tion continued for the hour it took to meander the three miles to the backstage entrance of the theater.

"Well, this is where my night ends." Ellis reached out a hand to shake Cinder's, but Cinder paused a beat too long for comfort before thrusting his palm into Ellis's warm, calloused grip. "I'm sure you've got more juice in you, but I've got an early morning. Thanks for an enjoyable night."

Cinder flexed his grip when Ellis made to pull away, keeping their contact for a moment longer before letting go. "Will I see you at the show tomorrow?"

Ellis hummed to the negative and shook his head. "I'm a rigger, remember? I'll be up in the fly space. I doubt you'll see me again before your engagement is over. I'm rarely on ground level when the band is present."

Panic flared in Cinder's gut. This couldn't be the last time he saw Ellis. The few hours they'd spent together were among the best he'd had in recent memory. He wanted more. Lots more.

But before he could ask that of Ellis, he needed to come clean about his identity.

Just not tonight. He couldn't ruin this perfect night. If telling Ellis who he really was put a wedge between them he couldn't budge, he refused to let it happen at the tail end of such a beautiful experience.

Which, in turn, meant he had to see Ellis again. As Henry. One more time.

"I get being busy during show time. So am I." Cinder shoved his hands into his pockets as Ellis rested one of his own on the door handle, his keycard gripped in the other, ready to let him into the building as soon as Cinder quit rambling. "But could we maybe plan to meet after? Or on our next day off—I mean, the next time the show's dark? After you're done"—Cinder motioned to the building behind Ellis—"here with your caretaking duties."

Ellis followed Cinder's gesture with his eyes, his grip tightening on the knob as his gaze landed on the backstage entrance sign. "I really shouldn't—"

The bubble of panic in Cinder's stomach moved to his chest, crowding his lungs until it was difficult to breathe. "I won't take no for an answer. Come on, man, we had fun, right? Help a lonely stranger to the city and keep me company. I promise I won't bother you at work if you promise to meet me somewhere after. Deal?"

Eyes shifting from Cinder to the door and back again, Ellis nodded. "Okay."

Relief flooded Cinder's system, and the tight band around his chest loosened. "Okay. Great. Can I have your number? Might make it easier to arrange things."

Wetting those plump lips until they shone like a beacon, stoking the flames of Cinder's barely banked desire with a cruel yet undoubtedly unconscious cry for attention, Ellis swallowed. Then repeated, "Okay."

Cinder didn't hesitate to yank out his cell, typing the digits Ellis offered into the messenger app on his phone and shooting off a quick text so Ellis had his number as well.

When they parted ways, Ellis slipping into the building with a final glance, a soft smile, and a farewell nod, Cinder damn near skipped his way to the parking garage.

His decision to stay in Vegas long-term was paying off at last.

Chapter Five

Ellis leaned his elbows on the handrail of the narrow metal catwalk overlooking the frontstage area and closed his eyes, allowing the music below to encompass him from all sides. Surrounding his senses. Filling his soul.

About three-quarters of the way through Cinder's set, there was a song that dripped with passion and heart, making exquisite use of his stunning vibrato. It had become a favorite of Ellis's almost from the get-go, most especially because its simplicity allowed him a moment to breathe, to open himself, and to fall heart-first into the music.

The constantly moving parts of the high-concept production ground to a halt during those three minutes and forty-two seconds. The fly space he occupied went still and quiet as a single bloodred spotlight focused on center stage, highlighting a lone wooden stool and a microphone stand. Following his third wardrobe change of the night, clad in skintight black jeans and a white ribbed tank, Cinder stepped onto the stage, clutching the neck of an acoustic guitar. As if on cue, the audience swooned into the orchestrated mood change.

They all knew what came next, and with a soft, collective gasp, the whole theater held its breath. Then, like the beat of a heart, as Cinder rested a hip on the stool, adjusted the strap of his guitar, and drew the microphone close, the crowd exhaled as one.

With the first note of the now familiar song, Ellis's chest tightened. Music had always held an important place in his life, affecting him in ways he couldn't explain. But nothing in his twenty-six years on this earth had ever latched on to his very being the way Cinder could with his haunting tenor as it trembled up an octave before plunging in both register and depth. Straight into his heart.

He looked forward to this brief respite more and more each day, surprised to find himself curious about the man who made such soul-moving compositions. Ellis rarely cared about anything other than the music itself, but something about Cinder's music was different. Something about *Cinder* was different; Ellis just couldn't put his finger on what.

Growing up in Vegas with a stepfather in show business, Ellis had never been impressed by celebrity. He admired the effort that went into reaching and maintaining stardom, but he could say the same thing about a lot of jobs out there. If someone put in a full day of hard work, they earned his respect, no matter what the end goal or result.

But Ellis's curiosity over Cinder wasn't based on the novelty of his fame or even over the man himself. It was the music Ellis yearned to delve deeper into. It affected him in ways he didn't understand, but he *wanted* to. It was like Cinder saw into a part of Ellis even he had never known was there, and he needed to know why... and *how*?

He wanted to put a face to the voice if only to prove Cinder was real. To prove the responses he drew from Ellis weren't figments of his imagination. To prove he was

still capable of emotions that ran so deep they could pene-
trate the walls he'd built around his fractured heart after his
mom's death.

To prove he could still *feel*.

Unbidden, Ellis's mind switched gears as the last few
husky notes drifted off and the stage plunged into blackness. Bright hazel eyes and a crooked yet charmingly confi-
dent grin floated into his thoughts, sending his pulse racing
and his own lips tugging into a smile.

Somewhere in the darkness below, Henry prepared
to join Cinder onstage. He'd never told Ellis what his role
was in the band, but Ellis could assume he was either the
lead, bass, or rhythm guitarist, considering his reason for
being at the theater on his off day was to rescue his forgotten instrument.

Prior to running into Henry for a second time the
night before, Ellis had gone out of his way to avoid looking
for him when the stage lights were up. Even though the
temptation had been there, he'd long ago learned to fight
the urges leading him toward self-ruin.

And yet, after spending an evening in Henry's company, Ellis was beginning to think the benefits of a friendship with Henry might very well outweigh the risks. Even
where his stepfather was concerned.

As the pulsing beats of the up-tempo song following Cinder's solo rendition vibrated through Ellis's chest,
he forced his thoughts away from the stage and into the
fly gallery. He had work to do, and unless Henry actually
made use of the number Ellis had given him the night before, miring himself in "what-ifs" about a future that might
not happen held little benefit.

As Ellis unbuckled his safety harness, all he could
think about was a cold shower and his bed. The show had

gone off without a hitch, but he had to get up early tomorrow to inspect the gridiron. One of his crewmates had noted unusual tension on a lift line, which meant he'd have to check every point of contact on the line set to be sure everything was in working order and to locate the origin of the hiccup before the troops arrived to prep for tomorrow's show.

"Did Dad tell you we've got another squeaky step on the front porch?"

Ellis startled as his stepsister's voice cut through his thoughts. He turned to face her crossed-arm pout with a forced smile. "Ah, hey, Suze." He still wasn't used to running into Suzette at the theater, but a few weeks ago, after completing her junior year of high school, she'd started working for their dad. Already, as a seventeen-year-old unpaid intern with only a fraction of the experience, Ellis's kid stepsister was leaps and bounds ahead of him on the career track of his dreams.

A fact she rather enjoyed rubbing in his face.

Stepping free of the leg loops on his safety harness, Ellis pushed his jealousy to the side. It wouldn't do him any good to stoop to the maturity level of an angsty teen. If he wasn't the bigger person, no one would be, not when Suzette was involved.

He put his safety gear away before turning and offering a genuine smile. Suzette's brows remained pulled into a grumpy V. When she blew a large pink bubble and let it pop with a loud snap rather than returning Ellis's greeting, he rolled his shoulders and sighed. "Dad mentioned the step last week, but I haven't had time to get home to look at it."

Suzette screwed up her face. "Can't you come by in the morning? Cin doesn't go on until evening. I'm sure you have time."

Cin? Ellis raised a brow. Had Suzette struck up a friendship with the talent?

He swallowed another wave of jealousy as his

thoughts wandered back to Henry for the umpteenth time that day. Ray would be livid if he found out Ellis had shared a meal with one of the band members, but Suzette didn't face the same restrictions.

It was crap, but that was Ray. He'd never forgiven Ellis for continuing to exist after his wife passed. Hell, he'd never much appreciated Ellis's existence in the first place. He'd always gotten in the way of Ray and Maggie's relationship.

At least, that's how Ray had seen it. Nothing Ellis had ever done—none of the endless attempts he'd made to get Ray to like him nor any of his countless efforts to simply go unnoticed—had ever been enough to win over the great Ray Brunswick.

For the first five years of Ellis's life, he and his mother had been an inseparable team. Ellis's biological father had died when Ellis was too young to remember, but the way Maggie talked about him, Ellis had grown up to idolize him as much as Maggie had. That is, until a new man entered her life, and rather than embody all the fatherly love and support Ellis had expected of someone taking the place of his departed hero, Ray had been... horrible.

But Maggie loved him, so for her, Ellis had tried. He'd ignored the glares and faces of disgust cast behind his mom's back. He'd put up with the tirades always aimed solely at him, even when they morphed from verbal attacks to physical ones when Maggie got sick. And when his mom died, he'd accepted the blame as readily as Ray had placed it on him.

He'd spent his formative years convinced he'd somehow made his mom sick and allowed her to die. Because he hadn't been *good enough*. Because he hadn't *behaved* as he should have.

And Ray never let him forget it. Even today, when his adult brain *should* be smart enough to fend off the irrational accusations, Ellis still let Ray get to him.

"*Hellooo.*" Suzette snapped her fingers in Ellis's face, jerking him back to the present. She squinted an eye. "Did you hear a word I said?"

Ellis sighed and massaged his temple. No, he hadn't, but he could guess what he'd missed, and it wouldn't make a damn bit of difference to how he'd respond. "Look, I'll do my best to get by the house on my next day off, but you might want to ask Ray to call a contractor. It might be a while before I can find the time."

Suzette popped another bubble and huffed through her nose. "It's *your* crappy old house. That means it's *your* job to fix it. You wanna pay someone else to do it, fine, but that ain't Dad's responsibility."

When she flounced off with a half-assed wave good-bye, Ellis dropped his head back and swallowed a groan. It was true. The house was his, although Ray certainly didn't see it that way. Nor did the bank.

When Ellis had taken on the job as caretaker at twenty-one and moved into his current living situation, his stepfather had done more than kick him out. He'd also threatened to sell the house. His mom's house. The only home Ellis had ever known, and the only physical space that still held memories of his mother. There was no way he could allow Ray to sell it, so he'd offered to take over the mortgage until he had enough credit to buy it outright for himself.

Which had proven harder than he thought it would, considering most of his meager salary went toward paying down a debt not even in his name.

Trudging toward the old green room for a change of clothes so he could shower off the funk of the day, Ellis pulled his cell from the side cargo pocket on his shorts and thumbed the unlock button. To his surprise, he had several missed text messages from Henry.

The first had been sent before the show started.

Hey. I doubt you'll see this until after we wrap,

which is for the best because you gotta stay safe up there, but I wanted to say thanks again for last night. Hope we can schedule a repeat... for tonight?

Another message had come through around the same time the last stage lights had gone dark. Before the house lights had even turned on.

Damn, I could really use a drink. Tell me you're free.

Ellis chuckled as he scrolled to the third message. This one had come in about twenty minutes prior.

I've been around the block enough to know you riggers work way too hard. I'm gonna assume you're still up in the sky and not just ignoring me.

When Ellis revealed the last message—sent only five minutes ago—with one final swipe of his thumb, his chuckle turned into a full-on laugh.

I'm showered and hangry. At this point, say no at your own risk, my man. I'll be waiting in the green room, but the longer you keep me here without sustenance, the more frequent and pleading these messages will get. I have no shame, and I'm not afraid to use that to my advantage.

Sighing, Ellis checked his watch and grimaced. Even if he wanted to—which, he definitely did—going out at this hour was out of the question. He had an early morning date with the gridiron and was already running on fumes.

To avoid an accidental encounter with Henry that might make his refusal all the more difficult, Ellis decided to skip the shower and head straight for bed. In the safety of his room, he propped his pillow against the wall and leaned into it before typing out a reply, cringing as he hit Send.

I wish I could say yes, but I've got a long day tomorrow. Rain check again?

There was a long pause before his phone vibrated in his hand.

That's cool. Sleep's important. I'll let you be tonight, but no promises I won't hop on the harassment bus again tomorrow. Stubbornness is one of my best virtues. You'll get used to it. Or you won't. Either way, it's still gonna happen.

Ellis frowned at his screen, wishing like hell he didn't have to say no, and praying the next time Henry *did* reach out—if there *was* a next time—Ellis wouldn't have to decline again.

Feed the hangry beast before it gets the better of you. G'night.

Barely a moment passed before those three little dots popped up, followed by a swift response that brought a ridiculous grin to Ellis's lips for reasons he didn't dare acknowledge.

Til tomorrow. Sweet dreams, E.

Chapter Six

66 Good thing you ordered enough food to feed an army, because I'm starving."

Cinder glanced up and smirked as his closest friend, Kumiko, and her wife, Lizbeth, sauntered into his dressing room. His DoorDash delivery—which they'd retrieved for him from the hotel's main lobby—dangled from Lizbeth's fingers, and Kumiko raised a questioning brow his direction. He motioned to the stainless-steel-and-glass coffee table with a jerk of his chin and returned his attention to the frustrating silence of his phone. "Help yourselves."

"Seriously, Cin, did you order the whole menu or what? You weren't planning a party you forgot to invite us to, were you?" Lizbeth dumped the bags on the table and greedily dug through their contents until she found something that piqued her interest. After snagging a set of plasticware, she flopped onto the couch beside him and dug into one of the countless pasta dishes Cinder had ordered from a local Italian restaurant.

Kumiko perched on the arm of the couch closest to Cinder and set to work kneading the tense muscles at his nape. "What's eating at you, boo?"

If anyone would notice Cinder's darkening mood as of late, it would be Kumiko. He sometimes thought she knew him better than his own parents ever had. Sighing, he closed his eyes and leaned into the much-needed massage.

On his other side, Lizbeth bumped his thigh with her own and added her two cents. "You know you can talk to us about anything, right? I mean, the godfather of our child is as close to family as it gets without counting all that genetics crap that means next to nothing in my book."

It took a beat, but her words sank into Cinder's addled brain and his eyes flashed open. He jerked free of Kumiko's touch and stood, whirling to face Lizbeth's grinning face and the playful exasperation flashing over Kumiko's regal features.

"Hold the phone. Godfather?"

Rubbing her palms on the soft cotton of her black yoga pants—her standard uniform outside of show hours—Kumiko darted a glance at her wife, who winked before stuffing another forkful of pasta into her mouth, then shifted her gaze to meet Cinder's. "Lizbeth is pregnant."

"She's..." Cinder shook his head, a grin tugging at his lips. "Well, shit. Congratulations, you two. That's huge."

Kumiko shrugged, then leaned across Cinder's recently vacated seat to brush an auburn curl off Lizbeth's brow. The pure adoration as their eyes locked in a silent but brief exchange was enough to flood Cinder with equal parts joy and envy. When Kumiko's attention returned to him, he schooled all the childish jealousy from his features and grinned. She beamed back and tilted her chin. "There's always a chance in vitro won't work, and those first few months of pregnancy hold so many risks. I hope you aren't upset we didn't tell you until now. We wanted to be sure it was really happening before we shared the news."

Cinder waved off her words with a flick of the wrist. "Don't you dare apologize. There is absolutely no reason you should've involved me in this. I'm thrilled to be let in on the good news now, but my third-wheel status *does not* stretch into your private marital life."

"I know, boo, but..." Kumiko sighed and stood, closing the short distance between them. She wrapped her slim arms around Cinder's waist, resting her head on his shoulder and humming in appreciation when he returned the embrace. "We love you. You know that, right?"

He nodded against her soft, silky cap of black hair, then kissed her crown. "I know, and I love you both too. Hell, apparently all *three* of you now."

Lizbeth groaned and leapt off the couch, abandoning her pasta as she darted over to join the love fest. She nestled under Cinder's outstretched arm and hugged Kumiko's waist until they fit together like the misfit puzzle pieces they were—reshaped by years of facing down the world as a united front until they'd molded into the inseparable trio they were today. "No getting sappy on me, you two. I'm a hormone monster right now. If you make me cry, you'll pay for it later."

Cinder hugged the two most important people in his life and tried like hell to focus on their joy and ignore the selfish twinge of anxiety their good news brought to light. They would never leave him. Motherhood might mean a new adventure he couldn't be part of, but it didn't mean he'd lose them altogether.

Still, with the growing number of personal pity parties he'd thrown himself lately, it wasn't a surprise his excitement had been dampened by his dual fear of abandonment and lifelong loneliness. They were at the forefront of his mind, after all.

"So." Kumiko poked a manicured fingernail into Cinder's ribs. "Our cat's outta the bag. Obviously, you're the godfather. You don't even get a choice to say yes or no, it just *is*."

"Yep." Lizbeth nodded against Cinder's shoulder. "And now that's out and decided, it's your turn to spill the beans. We're worried about you."

Cinder planted a kiss on both his girls' foreheads before stepping free of their joint hold and falling back to the couch with a heavy sigh. Lizbeth sat back beside him, curling her slender, tattoo-covered legs under her butt as she tackled the pasta once more. Kumiko chose the coffee table in front of him rather than returning to the couch arm.

He offered a half smile before dropping his gaze to the silent phone clutched in his hand. "Remember that guy I had dinner and drinks with last week?"

Kumiko nodded, her brows pinching. "Sure, the one you'd originally met during the kickoff party, right? Do we need to beat his ass?"

A laugh barked up Cinder's throat, and he shook his head. "No. It's just... I thought we had a connection. Something clicked, you know? I couldn't explain it then any more than I can now, but..."

"But?" Kumiko placed a reassuring hand on Cinder's knee. Beside him, Lizbeth wiggled her toes against his hip in her own silent show of support.

"He disappeared. Again. We exchanged a few text messages the next day, but then... nada. He doesn't answer when I call or text, and even though we work in the same damn theater, I haven't caught sight of him once since then."

Lizbeth nudged Cinder with her elbow, the one she referred to as her "Betty Booper" because of her penchant for shoving her bony-ass elbows into people's ribs, combined with her full-sleeve tattoo with the infamous Betty Boop at the center. "This despite hanging around here before *and* after the show, when the rest of us are out enjoying our new tourist trap of a home?"

He huffed out a small laugh. There was no sense hiding it from these two. They would weed out the truth one way or the other. "Yeah, even despite that."

"Is that why you ordered so much food?" Kumiko gestured to the two bulging sacks of assorted pastas on the table behind her. "So you could hunker down here while the show was dark and pray you ran into your hunky stage-hand?"

That was only partially true. The last time they'd had a break in the schedule was the night he and Ellis went out together. Every day since, there'd been at least one show. On those days with matinees scheduled, there'd been two. But now, after tonight's performance, they had two solid days off. Considering Ellis *lived* at the theater, Cinder planned to "run into" him after everyone else left for the night.

He'd ordered the massive quantity of food in hopes of convincing Ellis to share another meal together. He figured if the food was already there, and in plentiful amounts with every possible option available, Ellis couldn't say no.

Then maybe Cinder could find out why he'd stopped talking to him. If it *wasn't* because Ellis figured out Cinder's true identity and was pissed he'd withheld the information, he could remedy that mistake and any other he might've made to put a wedge between them. And if it *was*, he could beg for a second chance and any amount of undeserved for-giveness Ellis might be willing to offer.

Lizbeth dropped her head to Cinder's shoulder. "Why don't you come home with us? We could put in a movie, then bore you with our current list of baby names rather than letting you watch any of it."

Chuckling, Cinder gave Lizbeth's arm a squeeze. "I appreciate the offer, but I think I'm gonna hang here a bit longer, then call it an early night."

Kumiko stood. "Rain check for tomorrow?"

A band tightened around his chest at her choice of words. Ellis still owed him a rain check, and Cinder was de-termined to see it happen. "I'd like that." He stood and held out a hand to Lizbeth, who accepted his offer and allowed him to pull her to her feet. "Can I walk you ladies to the safety of your car?"

Lizbeth ruffled his damp, post-shower hair. "Anytime, cowboy."

Draping an arm around her shoulder, Cinder opened his other for Kumiko, and they headed for the door.

When they stepped out of Cinder's dressing room, a perky young brunette with a clipboard stood outside the door, pointing at something over her head and ranting at some poor soul hidden in the darkness above as they attempted to follow the snappish bark of her directions. Kumiko blew a low whistle under her breath, and Lizbeth hid a giggle, but all Cinder could do was frown and pity the recipient of her ill-tempered commands.

Surprisingly enough, when he returned twenty minutes later from the private underground garage where he'd deposited Kumiko and Lizbeth in their vehicle, Ms. Cranky Pants still lingered around his dressing room door. She clutched the clipboard to her chest as she popped her bright pink bubble gum and twisted a lock of stick-straight hair around one of her neon-pink polish-tipped fingers.

When she caught sight of Cinder, her eyes widened, and she sucked a half-blown bubble between her cherry-glossed lips. "Oh my gosh." She straightened her shoulders as her face brightened into a wide grin. "Hi!"

Without pause, Cinder slipped into his public persona, slapping on the practiced charm he'd perfected as a child and returning the young woman's beaming smile. But before he could say two words in response to her bubbly greeting, a movement out of the corner of his eye caught his attention. When he turned out of instinct, his eyes landed on a sweaty and beleaguered-looking Ellis, clad in a pair of cargo shorts, a sinfully tight T-shirt, and a safety harness that framed a certain part of his anatomy in a way that had the blood rushing to a similar location in Cinder's own body.

The brunette squeaked in surprise and darted to stand unnecessary sentry between Cinder and Ellis, holding her clipboard like a shield. Then, barely above audible, she hissed over her shoulder, "Get out of here."

No matter how misguided, Cinder appreciated the woman's attempt at protecting him from potential gawkers. But after waiting days to lay eyes on Ellis, and knowing, at the very least, his safety wasn't the reason he'd ghosted, Cinder wasn't about to let this pipsqueak human scare Ellis away.

"Ah, actually, I'd prefer if you didn't go anywhere just yet." Cinder locked gazes with Ellis, whose own eyes were wide with... surprise? Horror? A mixture of the two? "I've been looking for you."

Ellis swallowed. "You have?"

At almost the same moment, the brunette spun on her heel and frowned at Cinder, parroting Ellis's question with a much snottier version. "You *have*?"

With an awkward chuckle, Cinder nodded. "I have, actually. Any chance we could chat for a sec?" He looked at the woman and smiled. Patiently, and as kindly as possible, but with clear intent. "Alone?"

She raised her eyebrows and pursed her lips. "Of course." Then, before Cinder could motion toward his dressing room and invite Ellis inside, she turned her attention away from him and zeroed in on Ellis. "Be quick. We've still got work to do." Then she flounced away in a huff.

Ellis squinted one eye before dropping his gaze to the floor. "I'm sorry for not answering your messages. It's been a hectic week."

Relief washed through Cinder, lightening his mood significantly. At least Ellis didn't appear to be pissed at him. Maybe Cinder still had a chance to make things right. "No worries. You're here now."

"Yeah, ah, I really should get back to it, though. I'm still on the clock."

"Okay, so how about when you get off, we meet back here? I ordered some food. We could heat it up and—"

"I can't, I'm sorry." Ellis shook his head, a slight blush coloring his cheeks as he continued to avoid Cinder's gaze. "It's nothing personal, I promise, but you should really forget about me. You'd be better off looking for company elsewhere."

Cinder shoved his hands into the front pockets of his well-worn jeans. Something wasn't right here. If he believed Ellis didn't want to see him again, he wouldn't push the subject. He'd been on the receiving end of unwelcome advances far too many times in his life. No way would he force himself or his company on an unwilling party. But there was something else going on here. He didn't know *what* exactly, but he wasn't giving up that easily.

"I understand you're still at work, so I won't keep you. But do me one favor, okay?" When Cinder paused and waited for Ellis to lift his eyes before continuing, Ellis rewarded him with a look into those liquid crystal depths. "When you *do* get off tonight—I don't care what time it is—will you come by here?"

Ellis opened his mouth to protest, the objection clear in his eyes, but Cinder held up a hand to stop him. "No, I mean it. I've got food, a comfy couch, and a big-screen TV with every streaming service known to man. I plan to settle in for a chill night. *Whenever* your shift is over, give me a few minutes of your time, okay? Then I promise, I'll send you straight to bed for some much-deserved rest. Just... five minutes, okay?"

Biting his lip, Ellis darted a glance over his shoulder before sighing and offering a small nod. "Okay." When a booming voice called Ellis's name from off in the distance, he cringed and backed toward the sound. "I gotta go."

Cinder offered a small wave and a smile. "See ya soon."

Ellis paused, then lifted the corner of his lips into a

half smile in return. "See you soon."

Chapter Seven

Ellis put away his safety gear with slow, stilted movements. His brain hadn't stopped churning since his unexpected run-in with Henry.

He hadn't meant to ignore him. At least, not at first. But between the demands of his work at the Colosseum and the endless home repair tasks his stepfamily could come up with when they put their minds to it—like tightening the handle on a kitchen cabinet or patching a hole in the wall after Ray threw a full beer bottle at the TV when his team lost a big game—he'd had precious little downtime over the past week. The few times he'd checked his phone and seen Henry's missed calls and texts, he hadn't had the energy to respond.

Then Ray had dropped another bomb. In only a few short years, he'd managed to piss away all the money he'd received from taking out a second mortgage on the house. A second mortgage whose payment came out of Ellis's pocket right alongside the original sum.

Pairing Ray's alcohol abuse issues with a gambling problem meant his lucrative salary rarely stretched far enough to cover his excessive expenses. But when he'd taken out the loan, effectively saddling Ellis against his will with the hefty cost of supporting his addictions, Ray had sworn up and down it would be more than enough to get him out of the hole and keep him there. Unfortunately, he'd miscalculated his own abilities, and already his coffers had run dry.

There wasn't enough equity in the house to even consider a third mortgage—*thank god*—but Ray still expected Ellis to fix the issue. If he didn't, all the years of forking over damn near every penny he made to protect his home would be for nothing. And if Ray carried through with selling the house as he'd once again threatened to do, Ellis would not only lose that last tangible hold on the ever-fading memories of his mother, but he'd also flush every red cent he'd dumped into the house over the past five years, straight down the drain.

Then Ray had nailed one final jab by reminding Ellis that the future of his career rested in Ray's hands. If he lost his job at the Colosseum, something Ray could easily orchestrate despite Ellis's impeccable reputation with his direct boss and coworkers, no one in the industry would take the risk to hire him on. After all, there had to be *something* wrong with a twenty-six-year-old who'd stayed in the same entry-level rigging position he'd taken on as a fifteen-year-old high schooler.

Not to mention the fact that no one would even consider hiring him into any semblance of an audio position with no verifiable proof of his experience. Especially with his less-than-impressive work history.

It was Ellis's own damn fault he was in this situation. He'd been so blinded by his aspirations to one day fill his stepfather's gifted shoes that he'd believed every ounce of bullshit Ray spoon-fed him over the years. And yet, even knowing Ray hadn't meant most of what he said, a part of Ellis couldn't shake his underlying hope.

There was still time for Ray to follow through with his promises, and every time he placed a responsibility on Ellis's shoulders—to the knowledge of anyone else or not—it brought Ellis that much closer to the future of his dreams.

Ellis stopped at the restroom to rinse his face and hands, then stuck his whole head under the faucet and let the cold water drench his hair. He let it cool his overheated neck and trickle down his back. He needed a shower, but he couldn't keep Henry waiting any longer than he already had.

As much as he wanted to see Henry, Ellis was grateful Henry had only asked for five minutes. His muscles ached, his head hurt, and he had to wake up and do it all over again tomorrow. He planned to apologize for ghosting Henry and promise to make it up to him at a later, hopefully less busy, date. Then Ellis could steal a few private moments under a cleansing spray of water before taking a nosedive into bed and passing the hell out.

When he arrived outside the dressing room where he'd talked to Henry a few short hours before, Ellis squeezed his hands into fists.

Nerves had his pulse thrumming at his throat, which was utterly ridiculous. Henry was a musician, used to being on the road with ever-changing scenery and a horde of loyal groupies following him around like puppy dogs. Being stuck in one place likely made him itchy for something *different*. And what could be more different than striking up a friendship with a Las Vegas local who he believed could show him a good time and introduce him to Sin City's underbelly?

Not like Henry would be looking for anything more than that. Especially not from someone like Ellis. If Henry wanted a *true* friendship—or anything resembling the ridiculous desires swirling around Ellis's brain like a cruel reminder of what could never be—he could have anyone he wanted. Why would he choose a pain-in-the-ass nobody like Ellis? Someone who, despite his suffocating loneliness, didn't even have the energy in his overburdened existence to respond to a simple text message?

Sucking in a bolstering breath, Ellis knocked on the door with enough force to be heard but, *hopefully*, not loud enough to wake Henry if he'd fallen asleep. No need to add to his PITA status by disturbing Henry's much-needed rest, after all.

Within seconds, the door pulled inward and Henry stood on the other side, appearing far too sexy for his own good as he rocked the rumpled and disheveled look from his evening of lounging on the couch. Another reason Ellis couldn't let this "friendship" go any further—if Henry found out Ellis had the hots for him, things would only get worse.

"You came." Henry grinned, then before Ellis could respond, he reached through the doorway, snagged Ellis by the wrist, and tugged him inside. He led him toward the couch after toeing the door closed behind them. "I was beginning to think you were gonna stand me up."

Ellis allowed Henry to pull him down to the couch but immediately inched away, far too aware of the sweat and grime from his eighteen-hour day clinging to his skin, only amplified by Henry's shower-fresh scent.

"I can't stay long." Ellis shied away from Henry's penetrating gaze, instead letting his eyes fall to his lap.

"I know." Henry's voice was calm but forceful. In control. Somehow, with two innocent words, he managed to send a shiver of uninhibited desire up Ellis's spine. "I told you I wouldn't keep you, and I meant it. The show ended five hours ago, and you're just now getting off, so clearly, you've had a long day. I respect that. But I couldn't let you disappear again without at least getting an answer to something that's been eating at me all week."

When Henry remained silent rather than asking the question he'd hinted at, Ellis risked a glance up and found his gaze on level with Henry's. He'd pulled his bent knee onto the couch, facing sideways. His elbow rested on the back cushion in a casual lean, his hand dangling danger-ously close to Ellis's bicep. A single brow rose in question, further stoking the desire now simmering in Ellis's core.

Clearing his throat, Ellis straightened his shoulders and nodded. "Okay."

Henry took his time. His eyes bore into Ellis's, lock-ing him in place, as he edged ever-so-slightly closer. Near enough to brush the pad of his thumb over the two-day's growth of stubble on Ellis's chin, sending his heart rate through the roof.

Swallowing, Ellis fought to keep his voice steady when he rasped out, "I thought you had a question."

A half smile tugged at the corner of Henry's lips. "I did, and you just answered it."

"I did?" Ellis furrowed his brow. Lust clouded his thoughts, but he was still with it enough to know for damn sure Henry hadn't asked him anything.

Humming to the affirmative, Henry inched even closer. "I wanted to know if you felt the same way I do. I thought you might, but I needed to be sure before I decided how to move forward." His thumb returned to Ellis's chin, but this time, he traced upward until the calloused skin that went hand-in-hand with years of plucking a naked guitar string brushed the overheated and sensitive flesh of Ellis's lower lip.

Ellis clenched his jaw. He had to be misinterpreting the situation. There's no way he—

The thought cut abruptly off when Henry replaced the gentle caress of his thumb with the soft sweetness of his lips. A strangled groan escaped Ellis's throat, and he squeezed his eyes closed, his fingers curling into fists as he fought the urge to reach out and pull Henry against him.

As quickly as it began, it ended. Henry did little more than brush their lips together before pulling back, yet in the space of that single stolen moment, Ellis lost every ounce of his composure.

Fluttering his lids open, he furrowed his brow. "I... You didn't... I mean, I didn't think..."

A delighted bubble of laughter filled the air, and Henry's lips returned—far too briefly—to plant another chaste kiss over Ellis's. "You didn't think what? That I was gay? Well, you're right, I'm not."

Ellis shook his head, hoping the physical act would clear some of the fog from his brain. If Henry wasn't gay— if he wasn't interested in Ellis in *that way*—then why had he...?

"I can literally *hear* you overthinking." Henry huffed out a laugh, then knuckled under Ellis's chin and drew his gaze up to meet his own. "It's true, I don't identify as gay, but only because I'm not solely attracted to men. I'm pansexual. It's who a person *is* that gets my engine revving, not what body parts they have. And you, Ellis, are exactly my type."

A ridiculous flush crept up Ellis's neck, heating his cheeks until he couldn't maintain eye contact with Henry any longer. He wasn't experienced when it came to situations like this. Most of his adult life had been spent in a permanent haze of overworked exhaustion that left little time for socialization.

The few lovers he'd had were all from the years before he'd turned twenty-one, and none of them had been anything more than experimental curiosities. He'd figured out he was gay after puberty set in and the raging hormones that had his classmates salivating over the girls in their grade turned traitorous in his own body, leaving him squirming and awkward around the wrong sex.

But his mom—the one person he could've talked to about his confusing pubescent realizations without fear of judgment—had passed away before any of that hit. Talking to his stepdad was out of the question. So by the time he'd come to grips with his situation after years of inner turmoil and self-loathing, he hadn't known where to start. Out of desperation, as a nineteen-year-old virgin, he'd gone to a seedy gay club off the Strip and let some random stranger take him home.

Unaware of how clueless Ellis really was, the guy had unceremoniously rubbered up, slathered his dick in lube, and bent Ellis over the back of the couch three steps inside his apartment. Ellis had lost his virginity with his pants around his knees and his face shoved into scratchy, cigarette-smoke-saturated fabric. If that didn't sum up the extent of his "love life"—or lack thereof—Ellis wasn't sure what could.

"Okay, well, you held up your end of the bargain. It's been five minutes, and I got an answer to my burning question." Henry squeezed Ellis's knee before standing and reaching out a hand to help Ellis to his feet. "Just one more quick one and I'll let you go... Do you have a microwave?"

Ellis drew back his chin. "A microwave? Ah, yeah. I do."

"Good." Henry headed into the kitchenette area and dug into the refrigerator. He resurfaced with a large brown paper bag folded over at the top and nestled in a plastic grocery sack that read *Thank You, Have a Nice Day* in bright red capital letters with a yellow smiley face tucked between the lines of text. He handed it to Ellis, who accepted the mystery package with a grunt of protest. Henry pointed to the heavy bag, his lips curling into a soft smile. "It's Italian food. I ordered it for you—well, for *us*, but I've already had my share. Go ahead. Take it. Heat some up and fill your belly before you go to bed, okay?"

Bemused, Ellis could only nod as he let Henry guide him back to the door without a word of protest. But when Henry placed a hand on the door and dipped his head until their gazes met in order to stop him from mechanically grabbing the handle and exiting the room, Ellis frowned.

"Hey." Henry's own features creased in concern and his hands came up to cup Ellis's jaw. "Talk to me. Are you okay? Did I cross a boundary here?" When Ellis shook his head but couldn't muster a verbal response, Henry swore under his breath and dropped his hands. "I'm so sorry. I should've asked for your permission before kissing you. I should've—"

"No." Ellis forced the word past the constriction in his throat, shaking his head to emphasize the point. He swallowed a few times and ran a hand over his face. "You didn't do anything wrong." Ellis wheezed out a laugh. "I'm a bit rusty in this department. I need some time to process. This"—he gestured awkwardly between himself and Henry—"isn't what I thought was going to happen tonight."

Henry narrowed an eye. "No? What did you think was going to happen?"

Ellis pressed his lips together and shrugged. "I thought I was going to tell you being friends wasn't a good idea, walk out that door, and never hear another word from you."

Stillness enveloped Henry before he blew out a breath, his shoulders dipping a quarter of an inch. "Is that what you want?"

Ellis groaned and let his head fall back to stare at the ceiling, as if he could find the right answer printed on the corrugated drop tiles. When the water stains failed to prove helpful, he sighed and returned his gaze to eye level, focusing somewhere in the middle distance over Henry's shoulder. "No. I mean, yes, it *was* what I wanted. What I thought was best, at least, but now... I don't know."

"Fair enough." Henry's voice was soft and filled with understanding. "I know I've already demanded a lot of you today, but I have one more favor to ask, then I'll let you hit the sack without any more interference."

Spearing a hand into his still-damp hair, Ellis grunted his agreement but continued to avoid Henry's gaze despite the weight of his stare like a physical touch on Ellis's skin.

"Sleep on it. On this. On everything." Henry reached out to tug the door open, then stepped back to give Ellis room to make his exit. "When I text you tomorrow? Promise me you'll at least respond. I don't care if you tell me to fuck off, just... say something, okay?"

Overwhelmed with the sudden need to *run*, to seek space from the suffocating uncertainty gripping him by the throat, all Ellis could do was nod his assent before bolting to the safety of his room. Once again, in lieu of a shower, he crawled under the covers and hid from an emotional tidal wave brought on by a certain freckle-faced enigma.

Chapter Eight

For the tenth time in as many minutes, Cinder checked his cell for both an update on the current time and to be sure he hadn't missed a call or text from Ellis.

To his utter astonishment, without having to reach out to him first, Cinder had woken up that morning to a message from Ellis. A literal jaw-dropper of a moment, considering the endless calls and texts he'd sent into the ether never to be returned.

It had been short and sweet, but the meaning behind the words had Cinder's face splitting into a wider-than-normal grin, especially considering his precaffeinated state. He'd hopped out of bed like an ejector seat had launched his ass into the air and bolted for the shower.

As he'd waited for the water to heat in his over-the-top, shampoo-commercial-level-fancy chrome-and-pink-marble rain shower, he'd reread the message with a dopey smirk on his face.

I'm glad things went your way last night, not mine.

Before hopping under the spray, Cinder had typed out a quick response of his own.

Does that mean you'll let me take you to lunch?

As he ran a towel through his wet hair twenty minutes later, Ellis's reply came through.

I'd like that.

And now, two hours later, Cinder stood outside the backstage entrance where he'd agreed to meet Ellis. Even though he had a keycard to the locked door, he fought the urge to let himself inside and sweep Ellis into his arms for the no-holds-barred kinda kiss he'd held at bay the night before.

But it felt like an invasion of privacy, considering Ellis *lived* here and Cinder was there to pick him up for a date.

So instead, he kept his antsy nerves under control by checking his phone—again—to confirm it hadn't passed their agreed upon meeting time. Which it hadn't. Cinder still had five minutes to wait.

To pass the time, he practiced the speech he planned to give Ellis over lunch. The groveling, "please don't hate me for holding back the truth" talk he'd spent the entire morning honing into a carefully crafted mixture of one-part pleading, two-parts apology, and one-part *I did it because you're special, so please don't read anything nefarious into my actions when all I want is to get to know you better and maybe eventually strip you naked and* really *get to know you better.*

Although, he planned to read the room before testing the waters with that last part. Ellis had gotten skittish over a simple kiss, so Cinder needed to be sure they were on the same page before he made any further moves that direction.

The lock clicked and the heavy security door swung open, revealing the very definition of a sight for sore eyes. Cinder tugged down the bill of his pageboy cap to better shade against the harsh Las Vegas sun and drank in the tall glass of cool water dressed in a skin-tight graphic T-shirt, a pair of ass-hugging jeans, and scuffed work boots. Ellis's blond hair was still damp and combed back, but a few strands had already shaken loose and hung rakishly over his brow.

He smelled so sinful Cinder couldn't help the hum of satisfaction that worked up his throat when the scent drifted through the stagnant heat to settle over him like a welcome breeze.

Okay, so he had a crush on Ellis. A big one. It was both undeniable and entirely foreign. But... he liked it. A lot.

Almost as much as he liked Ellis.

"Hi." The shy smile that tipped up the corner of Ellis's sweet lips twisted Cinder's insides even further, until he ached for Ellis in a way he'd never felt before.

Was this what it felt like to be in lust with someone? Or had Cinder managed to skip past that stage without even realizing it? Because nothing about his feelings for this big, muscly softie seemed to fit the bill for simple *lust*. That was there too, of course, but when was the last time Cinder had taken a conquest out for lunch when they hadn't even warmed the sheets yet?

Hell, when was the last time Cinder had taken *anyone* to lunch who wasn't Kumiko or Lizbeth? He vaguely remembered the winner of a contest early in his solo career who he'd spent the day with as their "prize," but nothing else of note came to mind.

Yet here he was, about to take a man to lunch without any set plans for physical intimacy in the immediate future.

A self-satisfied grin stretched Cinder's lips as he shoved his hands into his pockets to ensure he kept them to himself. He'd wanted to make some changes in his life, and this was nothing if not solid proof he'd started down the right path. He still had a long way to go, but maybe Ellis could be the one to see him through his transition from self-centered strumpet to content and committed boyfriend.

Invigorated by the direction of his thoughts, Cinder returned Ellis's timid smile with a widening of his own Cheshire cat grin. "Hi right back atcha. Are you still in the mood for Mexican?"

Ellis nodded and straightened his back, causing the already snugly fitted fabric to stretch even tighter over the delectable muscles of his pecs, shoulders, and biceps. Cinder clenched his jaw to keep it from falling to the floor and gave himself a thorough mental lecture about the importance of not drooling down his chin on his first ever real date.

Cinder's jaw went lax as realization washed over him. He was twenty-nine years old and about to go on his very first *legitimate* date.

No pressure or anything.

Clearing his throat, Cinder tried another smile, this one a bit less cock-sure but hopefully lacking any hints of his sudden shift in confidence. "You wanna grab a cab or hoof it? It's hotter'n Hades, but Google Maps claims the restaurant is only a thirteen-minute walk, so if you're feeling adventurous…"

Ellis laughed and gestured toward the crowded sidewalk. "I think I can handle thirteen minutes in the brutal heat without melting. Check with me again after I'm filled to the brim with tacos and beer. Might be a different story then."

They fell into comfortable conversation as they sweated their way to the Cabo Wabo Cantina inside the Miracle Mile Shops at Planet Hollywood. After exchanging a few ideas, Cinder had landed on this touristy location—despite his initial plans to steer clear of such places—because he'd noted a shift in the way Ellis responded when the restaurant came up.

Sure enough, as Cinder held open the door so Ellis could duck into the cool haven of the Miracle Mile Shops,

Ellis admitted the laid-back, beachy restaurant with the Día de Los Muertos vibe had been a personal favorite ever since it opened in 2009.

Giving himself a mental pat on the back for reading Ellis correctly, Cinder followed his nose to the delicious smelling, jam-packed restaurant, immediately grateful his security team had made a reservation.

The ever-present tail had been a part of his life since birth, so he rarely thought anything of it these days. Still, he'd asked Emmitt and AJ—his primary detail—to keep a discreet distance so as not to make Ellis uncomfortable or intrude on their time together. That meant arranging things in advance with the restaurant to ensure the boys had a place to hunker down that wasn't up Cinder's and Ellis's backsides but still allowed them a clear line of sight to keep an eye on things.

As soon as the server sidled off with their orders, Cinder's stomach did a cartwheel. It was time. He needed to get the truth on the table before any more passed between them. If he wanted Ellis to see the same possibilities Cinder did for their future, they had to start building trust, not tip-toeing over the broken eggshells placed there by deceit and dishonesty.

"Listen, Ellis—"

"I wanted—"

They both laughed as their ill-timed attempts at kick-starting the conversation tumbled and fell over each other.

Ellis speared a hand through his silky blond locks. "You first."

"No, you, please." Cinder held up his hands in pure cowardice. He shouldn't let another moment pass with the mistruth hanging between them, but his nerve-ravaged gut grasped at the chance for a few more minutes of reprieve.

Ellis wet his lips with the tiniest peek of tongue that somehow still managed to be enough to send Cinder's brain spiraling toward thoughts of plundering that sweet mouth in search of his first real taste of Ellis. The chaste peck on the lips he'd restricted himself to the night prior had done more to amplify than sate his desire.

"I was going to say…" Ellis cleared his throat and glanced at the table, his eyes seeking a distraction in the glossy knotted wood of its surface. "I wanted to thank you. For last night." His eyes flashed up, latching on to Cinder's. "I never would've had the guts to kiss you first, but I've wanted to. For a while now. So… thank you."

Cinder's heart rate spiked, and a dizzying wave of pleasure washed over him.

Ellis had wanted to kiss him. *For a while now.* Cinder grinned. He could work with that. "Well, glad to help, but I hope there's no 'guts' involved now. If you want a kiss, all you gotta do is lay it on me. Capisce?"

Cheeks tinging a lovely shade of pink, Ellis opened his mouth to respond, but before he could, the server popped by to drop off a pitcher of frozen raspberry margaritas and two frosty glasses rimmed in sugar—a last-minute decision Cinder didn't regret one bit, especially when Ellis's eyes lit up as the icy beverage came into view. Cinder took the liberty of pouring them each a glass, then sat back and enjoyed the show as Ellis, grinning like a kid on Christmas morning, relished his first sip of liquid refreshment.

"Winner?" Chuckling at Ellis's dramatic eye roll signaling a clear *duh* response, Cinder reached across the table to clink their glasses before indulging in his first taste. It was smooth as sin and the perfect blend of sweet and tart. "Mmm, definitely a hit."

"Sierra Bravo, boss. Papa Charlie." Emmitt's familiar voice growled the dreaded code words signaling a *security breach* and *paparazzi close* into Cinder's ear as his tight grip wrapped around Cinder's elbow. "Gotta bounce."

Across the table, AJ had stepped behind Ellis, hovering close enough so on Emmitt's command—confirmed first by Cinder—they could usher the two to safety.

Dammit all to hell. Cinder closed his lids for the briefest of curse-fueled moments before locking eyes with a bewildered Ellis. "We've got some unwanted company. Paparazzi, which'll probably mean some fan action too. Mind if we get out of here before our margaritas wind up as front-page news?"

Furrowing his brow, Ellis glanced between Cinder and Emmitt, and then over his shoulder to AJ before nodding and pushing to his feet.

But their efforts were in vain.

"Ohmygod, it's *Cinder*!"

At the first high-pitched scream, Cinder dropped a slew of colorful swear words under his breath. So much for being the one to break the news. Ellis's confused stare bore into him, but every chickenshit bone in Cinder's body reared their ugly heads at the same moment, preventing him from making eye contact. Instead, he allowed Emmitt and AJ to take control and steer them through the obnoxious flashing bulbs, clutching hands, and endless blood-curdling screams.

By the time they'd found refuge in the security office of the Miracle Mile Shops, Cinder was convinced more than ever before that he'd royally fucked up.

Big time, epic levels of *royally fucked up.*

Chapter Nine

The hulking men who had shown up out of nowhere to escort Ellis and Henry through an anxiety-inducing throng of shrieking humans wielding cell phone cameras like weapons had shut them inside a small box of a room with an audible click as a lock on the *outside* slid home. Panic flared in Ellis's chest, stealing the air from his lungs, and cranking his heart rate to the max until it beat like war drums within his ears.

"I'm so sorry." The words wheezed from Henry's throat as he sank into a metal chair, its legs screeching across the cement floor. The sound was so like the screams still ringing in Ellis's ears it sent a chill down his spine. "I should've told you myself. I was *going* to, today, but... I should've done it sooner."

Ellis ran a clammy palm over his nape, massaging the tension from his neck muscles as he joined Henry in one of the rickety metal chairs seated at a peeling laminate top table in an otherwise empty room. Henry's words rattled through Ellis's brain, but he couldn't make sense of them. He couldn't make sense of *this*. Whatever the hell it was. "Should've told me what? What the hell was that? I don't understand what's going on."

Shame was the only thing keeping the anxiety at bay as Ellis struggled to ignore the fact they'd been locked inside this tiny little room and he didn't even know *why*. He wasn't proud to admit his fear of tight spaces—and of being confined inside them—had carried over from his childhood. This was a literal nightmare.

Henry groaned and dropped his head against the gray-painted concrete block wall. He lolled his gaze to meet Ellis's and frowned. "Those people were fans. And paparazzi. The men who hustled us away were my security team."

"Okay." Ellis pinched one eye closed, forcing his brain to *focus*. On Henry, not on the nerves firing willy-nilly under his skin, creating the unwelcome sensation of bugs crawling over his flesh. He needed to say something. Anything. As long as it kept Henry talking and the spotlight off him. "Do they always follow you to lunch? I mean, the security guys?"

Sighing, Henry speared both hands into his hair, knocking the pageboy cap off his head in the process. "Yes. I've had security following me around my whole life."

Ellis couldn't claim to understand the life of a rock musician, nor did he know enough about Henry's life outside the band to question why he would've needed protection as a child. But something about the way Henry huffed out the words through a pinched scowl caused Ellis's heart to constrict.

It was a much-needed reminder that everyone had their demons. Ellis's troubles were no worse than anyone else's, and he couldn't live his life dwelling on the trials of his past if he wanted to achieve greatness in his future—including allowing his fear of being on the wrong side of a locked door to get the better of him as a grown-ass adult.

"Ellis?" Henry reached out, and on instinct, Ellis placed his much-larger palm into Henry's grasp, smiling when their fingers intertwined. Henry returned his smile with a soft grin of his own, although it did little to remove the pain in his eyes. "Did you hear what they were screaming?"

Scrubbing his free hand over the barely-there stubble on his chin, Ellis thought back through the recent whirlwind that landed them here. One minute, he was enjoying the first sips of a delicious raspberry margarita—one of his favorite indulgences—and the next, two men he'd never met before whisked him and Henry away from their lunch, through the earsplitting but indiscernible shouts of a frenzied mob, and then shoved them into this prison.

Panic bubbled anew within Ellis's chest, and to keep the proverbial walls from closing in around him, he forced his attention on Henry's mouth. Those sweet, plump lips that had pressed so gently and fleetingly against his own and yet managed to elicit an avalanche of emotions with that brief moment of connection.

Without removing his gaze from the soft pink safety of Henry's lips, Ellis cleared his throat. "Ah, no, I guess I didn't."

Henry nodded and puffed out a breath, the force of which ruffled the flop of dark brown bangs no longer secured by his cap. "They were screaming Cinder." He swallowed and ducked his head, wincing as he said, "They were screaming my name."

Ellis paced the length of his cot and back again as the gears in his brain whirred in tune with the frenetic tempo of his heart. Henry—*his* Henry, the man who'd offered Ellis that sweet, unassuming kiss—was Cinder. *The* Cinder.

This could not be happening.

Thankfully, only a few moments after Henry dropped that bomb, the hulking guards returned. They'd laid out a plan to get Henry and Ellis out of the building without traversing through the mob again or spiking any curiosity elsewhere on their journey, but it required separating into two parties.

Reeling from Henry's admission and desperate to get free of the confined space, Ellis had jumped at the opportunity. He'd followed AJ—the guard who'd hustled him to safety at the Cabo Wabo—without sparing Henry so much as a farewell glance.

Not because he was angry with him, because he wasn't. Betrayal pricked at his heart, but with an intensity no worse than a bee sting. They barely knew each other, after all. Just because Ellis had opened his heart more than he should've didn't mean Henry had done the same.

No, Ellis wasn't angry with Henry. A little hurt, yes, but he could understand the rationale behind keeping his identity secret. What sent Ellis's stomach into nauseating flips had more to do with outside ramifications than anything on a personal or internal level.

When—not *if*, but definitely *when*—Ray found out Ellis had not only defied his orders to stay clear of the band but had actually gone on a *date* with the one-named wonder himself... He was so screwed.

As if on cue, a thudding knock shook the old green room door, and he braced for the inevitable. Somehow, Ray had already found out. Pictures taken by the paparazzi were undoubtedly circling the internet by now. Ellis's identity had been discovered. As a result, Ray had come to set Ellis straight. To remind him why fraternizing with the talent was such a bad idea. And why it would cost him dearly.

But instead of Ray's stocky form barreling into the room, temper flared and fist raised, Henry's voice carried through the door. "Ellis? I'm so sorry. Please, can we talk?"

What was Henry doing here? They'd only narrowly

escaped that mob, half of which had found its way to the Colosseum by the time AJ helped Ellis slip in the back. Henry should be tucked into the safety of his home, not circling back to the theater to face more chaos.

Ellis closed the distance to the door in one long stride. He tugged it open to find Henry with his hands shoved deep into the front pockets of his jeans, his face contorted into some complicated mix between a winced apology and anxious chagrin. "Thank you for opening the door. I know I'm probably the last person you wanted to see right now, but—"

"That's not true." Ellis sighed and stepped back, motioning for Henry to join him inside the room. The show was dark, but his coworkers often showed up on their off days to grab things they'd forgotten in their lockers or to get ahead on some egregious project or repair that had to be done before the next curtain call. The last thing he needed was for any of them to see *Cinder*, of all people, standing outside his door, looking for all the world like a kicked puppy.

When Henry accepted the silent invitation, and the door had been safely shut behind him, Ellis wandered over to his cot and sank onto its rigid surface. He planted his elbows on his knees and let his head fall into his hands. "It isn't your fault that you're, you know, *him*. I mean, you. I mean... *Cinder*." Cringing at his own stumbling word vomit, Ellis groaned. "I don't know how you deal with that mayhem on a regular basis."

Henry joined Ellis on the cot, which creaked and shuddered under the added weight. "It's part of the package. My parents are in the business too. It's all I've ever known."

Ellis lifted his head at this new tidbit of knowledge. When he met Henry's pinched gaze, he huffed out a laugh and dropped his hands. "I'm not upset with you. Don't feel obligated to roll out an apology on my behalf. I've dealt

65

with my fair share of groupies trying to break backstage or raucous crowds getting a little too riled up. I guess you're right in a way, that chaos is part of the business. I'm just not used to it being aimed, in any way, at me."

Rubbing his palms over the faded fabric covering his thighs, Henry shook his head. "I absolutely owe you an apology. More than one, actually. I never should've lied to you about my real identity. That was shady and dishonest and—"

"—and completely understandable." Ellis met Henry's quirked brow with one of his own. "You didn't know me from Adam, and if you grew up under the limelight, I imagine it was a shocker to run into someone as oblivious as I can be sometimes. No reason you should've called out my mistake in assuming you were part of the band and not, essentially, the whole band itself."

Henry licked his lips and stifled a sigh. "I appreciate your understanding. Really, I do. But I should've said something before I laid one on you last night. At the very least, before I asked you on a date. It wasn't fair of me to subject you to the bedlam that is my public life without giving you the option to bow out gracefully if it wasn't your jam."

"I knew what I was getting into." Ellis lifted his lips into a half grin when Henry tossed him a *yeah, right* eye roll. "I *did*, thank you very much. I knew you were part of Cinder's band, and I know Cinder is only the hottest rock star of our age." He chuckled when Henry dialed up the dramatics with the full-face version of his previous eye roll. Complete with a chin tuck and goofy, self-deprecating smirk. "You are. You know you are. Don't even pretend you aren't aware they call you the new Prince of Pop."

An unexpected blush highlighted that adorable spray of freckles before Henry darted his gaze to the floor. "If I'm so hot and *princely*, why didn't you know who I was?"

Was that a hint of insecurity coming from the self-avowed lifelong celebrity? Ellis couldn't help the full-belly laughter that snapped Henry's attention back lickety-split. "Oh, come on. I already told you I don't know faces or names. It's a character flaw. No need to rub it in. Plus"— he nudged Henry with his elbow—"something tells me you wouldn't have given me the time of day if I *had* recognized you. So maybe it's for the best that I was woefully ignorant to your Royal Highness's true position before now. Otherwise, there might've never been a *now* to begin with."

Henry narrowed his gaze, his head tilting in thought. "I'd like to think I would've more than given you the time of day, but maybe you're right. It was kind of nice to meet someone who I could trust wanted *my* company, not to be in the presence of someone they've seen in the tabloids. Incidentally..." He offered a ghost of his knee-weakening smile that somehow managed to be as sexy, if not more so, than the full-wattage version. "Henry's my real first name. In case you didn't know that. I didn't lie about that. Cinder's my stage name. A nickname, you know? Couldn't go around being the Prince of Pop with a name like Henry."

When he shuddered like the sound of his own name was somehow offensive, Ellis frowned. "I like the name Henry. Am I not allowed to call you that anymore?"

"You know..." Henry pressed his lips together, one eye twitching as he considered Ellis's question. "My parents don't even call me Henry. They embrace the glitz and glamour a little too seriously sometimes." He chuckled and angled his stare away, studying the ceiling for a moment before shifting back to meet Ellis's gaze. "I've kinda liked being Henry to you."

Ellis grinned and straightened his shoulders. "Yeah, well, I've kinda liked you being my Henry."

Chapter Ten

66That sounds beyond precious." Kumiko closed her warm brown eyes and hummed in appreciation, doing a full-body shimmy before refocusing her gaze on Cinder and grinning like a loon. "I can just picture this big, sexy stagehand tripping all over his words, trying to take back what his subconscious let slip."

Lizbeth, uncharacteristically misty-eyed, punched Cinder in the arm as she dabbed a napkin under her lashes. "*My Henry.* Oh, my heart." She released an exaggerated sob that held a little too much genuine gusto to not have a little bit of hormonal energy driving it home. "Kumi, our little Cinder's finally growing up. He's got himself a *boyfriend.*"

"It isn't like that." Cinder popped both brows. He hadn't expected them to get quite so dramatic and emotional when he spilled the beans about Ellis trying to backtrack his words when he realized his possessive slip of the tongue. At least, he hadn't expected it from Lizbeth. She was more stoic than he'd ever be. Or she had been. Until recently. Clearly pregnancy hormones were a bitch.

"Oh, isn't it?" Kumiko pursed her lips. "That otherworldly glow you've been rocking all afternoon and that radiant shit-eating grin you can't quite hide speaks otherwise, boo."

"Ellis and Cinder, sitting in the tree. K-i-s-s-i-n-g." Lizbeth barked out a laugh when her teasing rendition drew a glare from Cinder. Dancing lithely out of his reach, she snatched her wife's hand and spun Kumiko into her arms to finish the taunting song with a ballroom flourish. "First comes love—"

"—then comes marriage—" Kumiko winked as she joined in the game, allowing Lizbeth to twirl her around the patio.

"—then comes baby Cinder in a *baby carriage*!" Lizbeth shrieked with laughter as Kumiko took over the lead and waltzed them both into the dusty, cactus-filled backyard. The setting sun provided the perfect backlighting to frame the happy couple as they finished their dance to the tune of a song only they could hear. One that ignited a tangible desire between them so hot it rivaled the sweltering Vegas heat.

"And that's my cue to get the hell outta Dodge." Cinder chuckled as he got to his feet, scooping an armload of debris from their late lunch off the brushed copper patio table and heading for the sliding glass door that led to the cool reprieve of the air-conditioned interior. He wasn't surprised when Kumiko and Lizbeth didn't follow. He knew them well enough to predict with ninety-nine percent accuracy what would follow those smoldering looks they'd exchanged while gliding over the rock-strewn dirt, wrapped in each other's arms.

Something his own thoughts hadn't been far from recently, only starring a certain six-foot-three wall of muscle with the most adorable grin.

What Cinder wouldn't do to get Ellis naked.

He groaned and adjusted his belt. Now wasn't the time to let his mind wander that direction. Not only were he and Ellis not at that stage of their—whatever it was they had—but he didn't want to rush things. Ellis deserved better than that.

Only time would tell what their future might bring, but all Cinder knew was, he needed more. More of Ellis's sweet smile. More of his honest charm and calm, unassuming presence. More of their easy conversation and effortless amity. Quite simply, he needed more of *everything*.

Thankfully, he had that to look forward to in a short couple of hours.

After Ellis had, rather adorably, tripped and stumbled over himself trying to recant the *my Henry* that had slipped unbidden from his lips, the two escaped his dismal sleep space and set up camp in the remodeled green room. They'd ordered food from Uber Eats and spent the better part of the rest of the day falling down a YouTube rabbit hole because neither cared enough to turn off the auto-play feature. Wasting energy on searching for a video they wouldn't pay attention to didn't make much sense anyway.

It had been pure and total bliss. Cinder couldn't remember the last time—if ever—he'd shared such a wonderfully normal day with another human being. Hanging out with Kumiko and Lizbeth was anything but normal, seeing as how they both possessed fiery personalities and preferred to keep things interesting and new. The very idea of spending a lazy day in front of mindless television would be enough to set Kumiko's anxiety to full blast and bring out the Great Throbbing Vein of Irritation in Lizbeth's temple.

But with Ellis, it had been effortless. Simple. Filled with idle conversation and the occasional stolen touch. Nothing beyond the chaste trace of featherlight fingers over the back of a hand or an "accidental" brushing of their knees. But despite the mostly platonic appearance of their evening, lust had sizzled between them on a scale equal to or greater than any he'd felt between the doting lovebirds still spinning in their own little world under the pinks and reds and oranges of a gorgeous Vegas sunset.

Taking things slow was new to Cinder, but he had to admit there was something satisfying about the act. No momentary rush of physical pleasure had ever cranked his gears the way they'd whizzed and banged and smoked while he sat beside Ellis, fully clothed, with their legs kicked up on the coffee table. He'd never experienced anything as potent as the urges he'd fought to do something as simple as brush a kiss over Ellis's lips or explore body parts he'd never known were sexy until they belonged to a man he wanted but couldn't have.

Not that Ellis had come out and said Cinder couldn't have him. But there was a distinct sense of vulnerability and innocence lingering under the surface of Ellis's strong outward appearance. Until Cinder had a better handle on the situation, he intended to keep things as chaste as Ellis's actions dictated.

Because, for the first time, he *could*. And he damn well wanted to.

Without bothering to leave a note—his hosts wouldn't even realize he'd left until well after they woke tangled in each other tomorrow morning—Cinder bolted for his car. He tossed a wave across the street at the discreetly parked vehicle housing Emmitt and AJ, then hopped into his glossy black Jeep Wrangler, sans doors and roof, and headed for home.

Ellis had agreed to another date on their last night of freedom before the show picked back up, but when Cinder suggested they try Cabo Wabo again, or hit up another restaurant of his choice, the response had been less than enthusiastic. Which was why they'd settled on a change of scenery from the theater but nothing as adventurous as a public place. Instead, another delivery service food order had been placed and the two now sat side-by-side on Cinder's couch in the sprawling two-story living area of his very own home.

He was a bit nervous Ellis would be disappointed by another evening spent in front of the television, but he seemed as eager to veg out as Cinder was. Understandably so, considering, in order to make their date that evening, Ellis had gotten up at the ass crack of dawn to finish some project the theater owner insisted get finished before curtain call tomorrow. And since Ellis had his rigging duties to see to before the show, today was the only time he could do whatever the hell it was that was so blasted important it couldn't wait for another day.

Not that Cinder blamed Ellis. Not at all. He was a hard worker who put in an honest day's labor for everything he owned. Still, Cinder couldn't help but bristle at the idea of Ellis putting in so many long, difficult hours, especially when Cinder could gift him his annual salary ten times over without noticing the slightest change to his bottom line.

How was he supposed to reconcile such a hefty imbalance of wealth when Ellis insisted on paying his own way on their dates, and as a result of his need to work so hard for such a small fraction of Cinder's income, their time would be limited after today.

"You're awfully quiet."

Ellis's soft interjection halted Cinder's wayward thoughts and brought his attention back where it belonged. On the handsome man seated by his side. "Yeah, sorry about that. I space out sometimes."

"'S okay. Don't we all?" Ellis smiled and fidgeted in his seat, his fingers toying with the black and silver reversible sequins on one of Cinder's throw pillows. "If you're bored, we can always—"

"Bored? No way." Cinder shifted so he could face Ellis dead-on. "My mind wanders when it's given the space because I so rarely have free time to drift, that's all. It's nice. I'm thoroughly enjoying it. Especially with such high-quality company."

Ellis laughed off the compliment, but a faint blush colored his cheeks. "Same. To all of the above. Downtime isn't a frequent occurrence in my world, and the only people I ever really see outside of the theater are my stepfather and stepsister." His eyes darkened, his gaze dropping to follow the absent patterns he traced in the sequins. "They aren't really the best of company."

Stepfamily... but no mention of a birth parent or biological siblings. Cinder filed that away for later. He wouldn't press Ellis to talk about anything he didn't want to, but it was good knowledge to have. Cinder would have to be careful when discussing family until he knew the full story. The last thing he wanted to do was inadvertently strike a tender nerve.

"Do you see them a lot? Your stepfamily?" He aimed for casual with his question but hoped Ellis would pump the brakes if he needed to. To be safe, Cinder added, "You don't have to answer if you don't want to, of course."

Ellis shrugged but kept his eyes glued to the silver streaks slashing through black as he raked his fingers over the pillow. "More than I'd like to. They, ah, kinda both work at the theater."

"Oh?" Cinder couldn't help it, that news perked his ears. Had he met Ellis's stepfamily at one point? Hell. If he had, he really, really hoped he'd made a good impression. He didn't know where this thing with Ellis was going, but the butterflies doing a Cirque du Soleil act in his belly every time he so much as thought about him told Cinder he wanted far more than they already had. "Anyone I'd know?"

Another shrug and still no sign of those crystal blue irises Cinder couldn't get enough of. Instead, Ellis sighed and closed his eyes. "Ray Brunswick's my stepdad, and the brunette who tried to save you from me the other night? That's Suzette."

"Ray Brunswick? As in…" Cinder tried not to let the incredulity enter his voice, but seriously… the asshole audio engineer? *That* was Ellis's stepfather?

Ellis cleared his throat and finally focused his gaze back on Cinder. "Yeah, that's the one."

Cinder whistled. "Okay, well, that explains your mad skills at the mixing board. I'm guessing nepotism is somehow getting in the way of your career advancement?"

Licking his lips, Ellis nodded once in response. "The old man doesn't want to look like he's doing me any favors, but it's something we're working toward. Eventually."

Anger boiled under the surface, but Cinder forced it to a simmering scald. "Wait, isn't—what was her name again, Suzette?—isn't she working with him?"

"Yeah, but only as an intern." Ellis offered a half smile that didn't come close to reaching his eyes before once again casting that beautiful gaze to the floor. "There isn't a spot available for a full-time assistant. Every time one pops up, there's always a good reason why it isn't the right time. Ray promises he'll consider me again the next time one opens."

Ellis was quick to downplay the complete and total injustice of the situation, so Cinder followed his lead and kept a neutral expression despite the fury heating his blood. Instead, he took advantage of Ellis's downcast stare as an excuse to touch his stubbled chin, knuckling under it and lifting Ellis's face until their eyes met again. "I've spent my life surrounded by live music. I know a talented audio engineer when I hear one, and you, Ellis Tremaine, are one of the best."

When Ellis shifted under the weight of Cinder's compliment and didn't appear to have a response queued up, Cinder offered an olive branch in the form of a semi-topic change. "How old's your stepsister? She's younger than you, right?"

"Oh, yeah. About nine years. She's seventeen. She'll be a senior in high school this year." Ellis scrunched his nose. "She's not much better than her dad, to be honest. I pity the kid sometimes, though, because she had a rough go of things at the beginning. Ray kind of stepped out on my mom when she was sick, and he got his mistress pregnant. Then the woman dumped Suze into the system for a while before dragging her back out with the hopes of using their child to snag her hooks into Ray. Why she thought him worth all that effort, I'll never know."

Ellis let loose a mirthless laugh and slid further into his seat on the couch so he could rest his head on the back. "Anyway, by that point, my mom was gone, so they tried to make things work for a while. But Ray's not the easiest human to live with, and Suzette's mom was a hot mess. Eventually, she took off. Suze wound up under my stepdad's custody and never heard from her mom again."

Cinder swallowed, then risked a soft, "Your mom was gone?"

"Yeah, my ma died when I was nine. Ray had made a big show of offering to legally adopt me when they got married—mostly to appease his own ego, I think. He's not the kind of guy to want another man's child. He even tried to get Ma to change my last name to his, but thankfully she'd loved my old man and didn't want me to lose that part of him. Either way, by signing those papers, it meant Ray was stuck with me after she passed. He threatened to throw me into the system time and again, but luckily never followed through with it."

Ellis shook his head, as if trying to jiggle loose memories he'd rather not revisit. "Anyway, that's my childhood in a nutshell. Aren't you glad you asked?" His attempt at humor fell flat when his voice cracked at the end, and he turned away, the muscles in his jaw jumping as he clenched his teeth.

"All good superheroes have a sad origin story." Cinder picked up the thread of Ellis's jest with a small smile to match the one tipping up one corner of Ellis's sweet mouth. Cupping Ellis's cheek, Cinder leaned forward until their lips were but a hairsbreadth apart and whispered, "Can I kiss you?"

Instead of answering with words, Ellis's hands came up to frame Cinder's face, and in the blink of an eye, their mouths crashed together with the kind of passion and heat Cinder had only seen in movies or dreamt about on lonely nights on the road.

Their tongues clashed and swirled and danced with feverish abandon, their lips melding together only to be pulled apart and reformed time and time again. Teeth scraped over sensitive flesh. Hands, no longer relegated to drawing the other near, now had the freedom to touch and explore uncharted territory. Their moans and gasps filled the air around them until it became almost too much.

Cinder tore his lips from Ellis's, a cry of lust-fueled rage clawing up his throat. He wanted nothing more than to take Ellis right here, right now. To bend him over the back of his couch and lose himself in that beautiful man until they both forgot their own names and couldn't walk straight for a week.

But Ellis was worth more than that. He was worth more than a filthy fuck that stemmed more from in-the-moment desire than the care and devotion he deserved. Cinder wouldn't let his physical cravings get in the way of the promise he'd made himself under a cooler head.

Until he understood Ellis better and could put a finger on whatever caused that underlying innocence to scream *please don't hurt me* every time Cinder got close, sex was off the table.

Chapter Eleven

That familiar thrill as the opening notes of "Heartbeat Away" soared into the fly space had Ellis abandoning his current task and heading for his favorite viewing place. If he stood in the right spot, he could watch Henry saunter onstage under the veil of that moody red glow. Then, as Henry sank onto the stool and slipped the strap of his acoustic guitar over his head, Ellis could close his eyes and let the music wash over him.

It was different now than it had been before he'd known Cinder and Henry were the same person. Not better per se—because Cinder's voice had melted Ellis's heart from the beginning—but with that touch of something personal added in, the words sank a little deeper and his silky vibrato resonated a little stronger.

There was no mistaking the desire sizzling through the air every time they were together, like white-hot sparks of electricity arcing between two naked wires. But for some reason, Henry kept things frustratingly casual and friendly.

The closest they'd come to anything resembling the physical contact Ellis craved had been that one and only make-out session on Henry's couch over two weeks ago.

The brilliant perfection of the moment had lasted all of thirty seconds before Henry very gently and very succinctly put an end to it. But everything about the way Henry looked at Ellis, his eyes darkening until the amber and chocolate tones overtook the green almost completely, spoke to a yearning for more. As did the way his lips curled into a smile when they were alone, all soft and secret. A version of that famous grin he reserved for Ellis and Ellis alone.

And yet, despite all the signs of mutual attraction, Henry remained out of reach, and Ellis couldn't bring himself to make a move. He'd never been one to take control, especially in situations where he couldn't be positive all parties wanted the same thing. After all, if Ellis was reading the situation correctly, wouldn't Henry take what he wanted? He hardly seemed the shy wallflower type. That was Ellis's wheelhouse.

Still, despite the distinct lack of anything resembling physical intimacy, there was *something* blossoming between them. Ellis couldn't bring himself to believe he was alone in the feelings taking root in his heart.

Was it the beginning of love? Or unrequited lust? He couldn't say for sure. He hadn't loved anyone since his mother, and he and Henry had only known each other for a few weeks. Longer, really, if Ellis counted that night in the sound booth two months ago as the start of whatever this was. When—backlit by Ballyhoo lighting and set to a soundtrack he'd cultivated himself—he first laid eyes on the man who nearly consumed his every waking thought.

Despite Ellis's hefty work schedule, they managed to find a little time together every day. In the remodeled green room or Henry's dressing room after a show, and Henry's living room on the few nights the show had been dark. They'd pretend to watch TV or random YouTube videos, but their focus always remained on each other. Talking. Laughing. Stealing innocent touches but never anything more.

Another two-day blackout kicked off after tonight, and Henry had invited Ellis to spend most of that time with him. The only thing keeping Ellis from packing a bag and holing up in Henry's desert estate for the entire duration was his caretaking duties and a massive rewiring endeavor Ray had dropped in his lap the day prior.

As long as there weren't any unexpected surprises when he dug into the project, he hoped to get enough of it done during the day tomorrow to allow for an early start to his and Henry's evening. One he hoped would stretch well into the night and end with them naked and sweaty on Henry's bed.

Gods willing.

The rest of the show flew by as Ellis oversaw the fly galley, stealing glances when he could at the stage below. By the time he'd wrapped up his duties, he found Henry waiting for him in the green room—as he always was after the show now. Come hell or high water, no matter how exhausted he had to be after spending hours under those oppressive stage lights fronting a very physical act, Henry was there.

Ellis flopped down on the couch and let his head fall against the cushioned back. He turned his neck so he could see Henry, who lounged against the arm facing Ellis, a grin stretching his lips. Ellis matched his smile as he kicked his feet up on the coffee table. "Congrats on another great show tonight."

"You deserve as much credit as I do." Henry held up a hand before Ellis could even contemplate the argument that statement deserved. "Do you think front stage divas operate in a bubble? We couldn't do what we do without all of you backstage magicians keeping things running smoothly. You're as much a part of the show as I am."

Barely suppressing the wry grin tugging at his lips,

Ellis sighed and shook his head. "If I didn't see you on that stage every night with my own two eyes, I'm not sure I'd believe you were really Cinder."

Brow furrowed, Henry grunted, "Huh?"

Ellis rolled his head so he could stare at the ceiling instead of into those probing hazel eyes. "You're so down-to-earth and genuine. It's hard to imagine someone with Cinder's level of lifelong celebrity as a real, everyday human. Sometimes it feels like who you are on that stage is your superhero alter ego, but that underneath, you're really just Henry." Ellis licked his lips. "*My* Henry."

The last time Ellis had said those words, he'd done everything he could to backpedal. Although part of him hadn't yet acknowledged he wanted them to be true even then, the mere thought of making such a bold claim without being sure Henry felt the same was terrifying.

And yet, here he was. Doing it again.

Oh god. What was his problem? It was no wonder Henry wasn't looking for a physical relationship with him. He was an anxiety-riddled mess. Henry had probably decided long ago to keep things simple between them out of fear Ellis might melt down and have an epic panic attack during sex.

"Ellis?" Henry's voice had dropped an octave and filled the room with its rich, buttery-softness. "Will you look at me, please?"

A tiny flicker of fear had lived within Ellis ever since childhood. Like a pilot light burning at his core, ready to ignite into a fiery ball of anxious terror at the slightest provocation. When he turned to face Henry, the heat of impending dread clawed at his chest, taking up residence beside the panic. But the moment their eyes met, and Henry closed the daunting chasm between them by taking Ellis's hand and threading their fingers together, the flames of turmoil subsided.

Henry searched Ellis's eyes, holding tight to his hand

as if he somehow knew his presence and touch were the only things keeping Ellis's head above water. As if he could see straight through to every broken piece of Ellis's soul, clinging to sanity by a thread that grew weaker every day.

"Shh. It's okay. Come here." Again, Henry's voice broke the silence. Soft and placid, yet firm and no nonsense. He guided Ellis's head into his lap and stroked the hair off his forehead. "Breathe for me. Nice and easy. In and out. There you go, just like that."

Ellis closed his eyes and focused on Henry's touch as he tenderly carded his fingers through Ellis's hair. The tightness in his chest and the swirling numbness in his brain ebbed away, replaced by the warmth of Henry's thigh beneath his cheek and the rhythmic stroking of Henry's fingers over his scalp.

In some distant part of his brain, a thought drifted in and out of his consciousness. A realization that this must be what it felt like to be loved. To be cherished and cared for by someone who put his safety and mental health above all else. But as quick as it entered his mind, it was gone, and he let himself float on the endorphins rushing through his system instead.

When his heart rate had returned to normal and the sound of water rushing in his ears no longer separated him from the world around him, Ellis opened his eyes. He couldn't see Henry's face, but those comforting fingers still worked through his hair, and the steady strength of his thigh remained sturdy beneath Ellis's cheek.

Ellis couldn't remember the last time he'd felt so serene. Centered. *Complete.*

"Feeling better?" Henry murmured the words, his hand moving down to massage Ellis's nape.

Turning his head, Ellis found Henry's penetrating gaze waiting. Watching. Searching Ellis for the sign of another breakdown, no doubt. But when Henry straightened his shoulders, bringing himself back to his full seated height, something coiled in Ellis's chest. Tightening, but in a good way.

It was an entirely new sensation, but one he could get very, very used to.

Henry stood then, holding out both hands to help Ellis to his own feet. But before Ellis took him up on the offer, his eyes traveled the length of Henry's leanly muscled body until they met Henry's own.

A single brow popped in question as Henry dropped his hands. "You okay?"

It made no sense, but with Henry looking down on him with so much concern and care, Ellis felt more secure and protected than he ever had. Swallowing, he rose to his feet without Henry's help, their locked gazes never breaking. "I'm... Yeah. I'm good. Really good. Thank you."

Henry wet his lips, drawing Ellis's gaze immediately south to their pink softness.

"Ellis?" Transfixed on Henry's yielding mouth and the subtle way it formed his name, Ellis could only grunt in response. Henry chuckled and stepped forward until their closer proximity paired with their six-inch height difference forced Ellis's lowered gaze to move up Henry's face until their eyes met again. "I want you to feel safe with me. Is there anything I can do—or *not* do—to make you more comfortable?"

That snapped Ellis's attention back full tilt. "I do feel safe with you." His nerves threatened to surface again, but Ellis forced them back down. He couldn't let Henry think he was uncomfortable around him or, gods forbid, that he didn't feel *safe*. He was a grown-ass man. *Jesus*. He'd made quite the impression these past few weeks, hadn't he?

Sinking back to the couch, Ellis speared both hands in his hair and groaned. "I'm sorry for being such a mess. I swear, it isn't you. There's nothing you can do to fix what's wrong with me, and there's certainly nothing I'd want you to stop doing. If anything..."

When Ellis closed his eyes on a silent self-loathing curse for daring to start that sentence, Henry sat down beside him and placed a hand on his knee. "If anything...? Go on. You can talk to me about anything. I promise, I'll be the last person to judge. I grew up on the road. Touring isn't good for one's mental health sometimes, so I've seen my fair share of struggles. Hell, I've been the one struggling more times than I can count. I might not understand exactly where you're at, but I can probably put myself in a pretty similarly sized pair of shoes."

With a sigh, Ellis dropped his hands and shook his head at his own stupidity. "I was going to say, if anything, I wish you'd do *more*." He arrowed a look at Henry, whose brows had drawn into a V. "We've been dating or whatever you want to call this"—he motioned between himself and Henry—"for at least two weeks now. We had one insanely hot kiss almost as long ago and then... nothing. I mean, if you aren't interested in me that way—"

"Whoa." Henry squeezed Ellis's knee. "No. No way. I'm extremely interested. It's not that. Not at all."

Ellis huffed and leaned back, crossing his arms like the petulant child he was trying to prove he wasn't. "Then what are we doing? Or more specifically, why *aren't* we, you know, 'doing'?"

Henry pinched the bridge of his freckled nose. "It's a bit complicated, and I'm worried you'll be upset with me, but... I've been waiting for you to make the first move. I kind of got the impression something was... I don't know. I didn't want to force you into anything you weren't comfortable with. I'm completely happy with where we are. There's no rush to get physical on my end."

"Isn't there?" Ellis scrunched his nose. "You're an international rock star. I'm sure you're used to having sex whenever and with whoever you want."

Sighing, Henry turned on the couch until he could face Ellis more easily. "I'm twenty-nine years old. Sure, I lived that life. Probably for longer than I should have and certainly longer than I wanted to, but I'm ready for something more. The whole reason I took this gig was to put down some roots for longer than the few weeks it takes to record an album before flying off on another tour."

Henry took Ellis's hand and pulled it into his lap so he could cradle it between both of his own. The juxtaposition of his slender, black-polish-tipped fingers beside Ellis's larger, work-hardened digits was oddly comforting. "I mean it when I say what we have right now is everything I want and more. I've never had the chance to get to know someone the way I'm getting to know you. Hell, I've never actually dated anyone before. Please don't think I'm not loving every minute with you, exactly as it is. Promise me that, okay? Please?"

Ellis swallowed and pressed his lips together to stop the quiver of emotion from showing. "I do. I understand that. And I feel the same way." He screwed up his face and looked away. "I'm sorry for making you think I wasn't comfortable with you. Or that you couldn't, you know, touch me. It isn't you, and I absolutely *want* to have sex with you. I just..."

Should he tell Henry why he was so jumpy? Or why he sometimes pulled away when he really wanted more, not less, of Henry's touch?

Or should he keep his mouth shut and hope Henry didn't ask any more questions?

"You just what, Ellis?" Henry threaded their fingers together and drew their joined knuckles to his lips for the softest breath of a kiss. "Tell me what's circling around that brain of yours. Don't make my decisions for me. I know what I can and can't handle, and I promise you, I can handle anything you have to say. *We* can handle it. Together. Whatever it is."

Ellis rolled his shoulders but kept his gaze averted. "I had a—*difficult*—childhood. Ray wasn't the easiest stepfather to have around, and after my ma died, things got worse. He wasn't thrilled that he wound up stuck with me and liked to take out his anger and disappointment with his fists."

Chuckling, more out of awkward discomfort than any semblance of humor, Ellis continued through gritted teeth, "Even though I don't live with him anymore, Ray's still a big part of my life. I... I still have to see him all the time. It screws with my head sometimes, and I don't always deal super well with some situations. Because I'm a coward. In a lot of ways, I'm still that scared little boy waiting for the next beating to come."

He turned to meet Henry's gaze; his jaw now clenched in defiance rather than humiliation. "The thing is, I feel safer and happier when I'm with you than I have in longer than I can remember. I've never been good at taking charge or asking for what I want, but I want *you*, Henry. I *need* you."

A soft, crooked smile tugged at Henry's lips, and he lifted a hand to cup Ellis's jaw. "I want you too, baby. And with your permission, I'd be happy to take control."

Chapter Twelve

Cinder sat on the arm of the couch, legs kicked out and crossed at the ankles, arms folded over his chest. His eyes focused on his closed dressing room door, willing it to open.

He'd sent Ellis to the showers over twenty minutes ago after being denied access to even a kiss without allowing Ellis a chance to clean up first. Considering Cinder had waited over two months to unwrap the gift of Ellis's delectable body, he figured he'd be a bit more patient with the deed imminent.

However, the more time that passed, the more worried Cinder grew that Ellis had changed his mind and was trying to come up with a way out of his previous declaration. Which meant Cinder would need to be extra careful and watch closely for any signs of second-guessing or regret.

He'd known there was something deeper going on with Ellis, something that made him fidgety and skittish and grow tense any time Cinder got too near. He'd guessed it might have something to do with that bastard Ray Brunswick, but it broke him when Ellis admitted to a childhood of abuse and neglect at the hands of a man who continued to hold a position of power over him, both on the job and, apparently, in his personal life as well.

After all, the whole reason Ellis had been so upset over their close call with the paparazzi a few weeks ago, and why their relationship had been relegated to a secretive affair out of the public eye, was because Ray had threatened Ellis. Why, Cinder still didn't fully understand, but when he saw the genuine fear in Ellis's eyes, he hadn't thought twice about doing as he'd asked. As long as he got to spend time with Ellis, he didn't care if they had to do so behind closed doors.

For now, at least.

He didn't need to broadcast every part of his private life to the world, but if things kept going the way they were, Cinder wouldn't be able to hide Ellis forever. Hell, he wouldn't want to. Not if his heart kept traversing down its current path. He was already struggling not to shout his feelings from the highest rooftop—of which there were plenty to choose from in Vegas—and he hadn't even fallen in love yet. At least, he didn't think so.

Was a single kiss and countless hours spent just outside of easy touching range enough to send a heart plummeting off the cliff toward love?

He certainly wouldn't know. After a lifetime of booty calls and one-night stands, this thing with Ellis had him tiptoeing through unknown territory from damn near day one. Which only made Ellis's revelations earlier all the more difficult to swallow. When Cinder was already going into this thing blind from every angle, how was he supposed to handle Ellis's traumatic past?

It didn't scare him, and it certainly didn't make him think any less of Ellis. But it *did* put some added pressure on Cinder to get his shit together and be the man Ellis needed.

No, the man he *deserved*. Cinder couldn't fly by the seat of his pants anymore. He had to start putting someone else fully above his own needs, and that meant understanding Ellis better so he could estimate the best path forward for them both.

It also meant listening to Ellis's *wants* even when they didn't line up with Cinder's understanding of *right*. Like the fact Ellis refused to let Cinder get that worthless alcoholic stepfather of his fired despite him being more than deserving of the treatment.

Cinder closed his eyes and took a deep, cleansing breath to center himself. The last thing Ellis needed after admitting to suffering post-traumatic stress from a harrowing childhood was for Cinder to approach their first physical act together with anger boiling under the surface.

As the doorknob he'd spent the better part of the past twenty minutes staring at finally jiggled and turned, Cinder made a split-second decision. A damn good thing he did too. If he hadn't made up his mind before Ellis stepped into the room wearing nothing but a pair of worn jeans slung low around his narrow waist, Cinder would've taken him right then and there. And it wouldn't have been what Ellis deserved.

"Hi." Ellis smiled, a shy blush tinging his cheeks a rosy pink. The chiseled torso Cinder had fantasized about more times than he could count still bore several beads of water—remnants from his shower. "Sorry it took so long. I had a bit of an existential crisis."

Shit. As he'd feared. Cinder stood and closed the distance between them, locking his gaze with Ellis's even though enough blood had rushed south to split his brain control in two. He stopped short of suffocation distance and tipped his chin so he could maintain eye contact with the Greek god towering over him.

Focus, you jackass. "Talk to me. What happened?"

Ellis curled his lower lip in and shrugged. "It dawned

on me that I spewed some pretty unmanly nonsense back there. I wanted to give you some time to make an exit if you changed your mind about... this." He lifted his arms and motioned to himself before dropping them with a self-deprecating smirk. "I haven't really mastered the art of being sexy. Seems I've got a long way to go."

"Oh, baby." Cinder clenched his fists to keep from reaching out before he knew for sure where Ellis's head was at. "Nothing that happened in your childhood was your fault, and the fact that that asshole continues to manipulate and intimidate is on him, not you. He knows what he's doing because he knows what he *did*. He's using the awful things he did to you as a child to his advantage, but nothing about that makes you any less *manly*. Certainly, no less *sexy*."

Cinder tilted his head, keeping his countenance as casual and nonthreatening as possible. "Can I touch you?"

Brows popping, Ellis simply nodded and melted into Cinder when he closed the final few inches separating them. As soon as they came together, Ellis released a quivering breath that tickled the sensitive skin behind Cinder's ear.

Wrapping an arm around Ellis's waist, Cinder pressed his hand flat against the middle of Ellis's lower back to keep their bodies flush. With his other, he guided Ellis's mouth down to meet his own, finally drinking from those lips with the unreserved abandon he'd yearned for after that tantalizing sample still haunting his happiest reveries and filthiest dreams.

Ellis's strong arms folded around Cinder, tugging him close and holding him there as they both took their fill. Eventually, Cinder found the strength to separate their lips, but only long enough to gasp, "Okay?"

With an animalistic growl, Ellis dipped his knees, placed a hand behind each of Cinder's thighs, and lifted him into his burly arms. He nuzzled his stubbled face under Cinder's jaw, his hot breath fanning over Cinder's neck. "I've wanted this from the moment I first tasted your lips."

Cinder gripped Ellis's shoulders as Ellis walked them both over to the couch and eased Cinder onto his back, covering his body with the solid heat of his own. When Ellis rocked his hips and their cocks grazed together through two layers of denim, Cinder's fingers dug in deeper, a hoarse wheeze escaping his throat.

Perhaps he'd been missing more than he realized by always choosing to be the bulkier body in his sexual pairings. There was something inexplicably delicious about being surrounded and maneuvered by someone with so much *strength*.

Cinder pressed his lips to Ellis's throat and swirled his hips to increase the friction. A shared moan filled the air before Cinder slid a hand down to cup Ellis's rock-hard backside and murmured into his ear, "I want you naked."

Ellis nodded against Cinder's shoulder, his panting breaths a thing of beauty as he fought to maintain some semblance of self-control. The jerking, hungry motions of his hips spoke in tandem to his crumbling restraint.

But despite the frenzied passion driving his body to visibly scream for more, Ellis submitted to Cinder's request without hesitation. He levered off Cinder until their eyes met. A twinkle of desire sparked between them, laced with something more. Something Cinder would unpack and examine later, but that flitted away quickly enough to leave his attention zeroed in on the physical yearning drawing them together like a magnet to metal.

Ellis stood beside Cinder, who remained splayed out on the couch. With a sexy smirk pulling at his kiss-plumped lips, Ellis flicked open the top button of his jeans and gave the zipper a tug. Rather than revealing the soft cotton of underwear, a well-trimmed thatch of golden-blond hair peeked through.

Cinder sucked in a breath and pushed up to his elbows. "Lose the jeans, baby."

Smirk growing more pronounced, Ellis hooked his thumbs into the front pockets of his jeans and tugged until they fell into a pool at his feet. Kicking them free, he spread his arms and allowed Cinder to soak up the full, stunning glory of Ellis bared.

"Christ, you're beautiful." Cinder's voice came out gravelly and hoarse as his gaze traveled every inch of Ellis's body. Greed and the ache of ravenous desire drew a snarl up his throat. Swinging his legs around so he now sat on the couch rather than lying upon it, Cinder spread his knees and motioned Ellis forward with a crook of his finger. "Come here, big boy."

The hesitation was brief but evident—a shift, really, from one headspace to another as Ellis closed the distance to stand before Cinder. His swagger faded, and in its place was the shy, blushing submission Cinder had grown used to seeing in Ellis.

But he wouldn't assume anything. He would ask, and he would verify. Over and over again. As many times as it took until the necessary trust and instinctual, mutual expectations had been established. "Can I touch you?"

Ellis sucked in his bottom lip and blew out a heavy, shaking breath through flared nostrils. He nodded, his eyes glazed with wanton anticipation.

Cinder placed his palms over Ellis's hipbones and rubbed his thumbs in gentle circles over the soft skin there. Ellis stuttered out a moan, and Cinder locked their gazes. "Lace your fingers behind your head and close your eyes. I want you to focus entirely on the sensation of my hands on you. On the sound of your own labored breaths. Can you do that for me?" Ellis's eyes widened, but he nodded and lifted his arms to thread his fingers together against the back of his neck. Cinder lifted his chin, his brow raised in silent question. "And you know I'll stop if you ask me to, right?"

His own brows wavering in a delightful mixture of

confusion and humor, Ellis nodded again. "Of course. Although I can't imagine a reason I'd ever ask you to."

Pursing his lips, Cinder could only shrug in response. Perhaps someday they'd explore Ellis's boundaries, but today would not be that day. "Close your eyes, baby."

Obeying the command without another moment's hesitation, Ellis shifted his feet to widen and steady his stance, inadvertently bringing his dick to perfect mouth height. Cinder licked his lips but shoved that thought aside for now. Until they were tested, unprotected contact wasn't smart, and he didn't have a condom within easy reach. Perhaps more important, he hadn't asked Ellis's permission for oral contact.

Instead, Cinder traced his fingers over the ludicrous Apollo's belt etched into Ellis's lower abdomen and reveled in the way Ellis's breath hitched at the touch. He skated over every inch of warm, golden skin he could reach, following the lines and angles of perfectly sculpted muscles. When Cinder's attention strayed to the crease of Ellis's groin, working toward the evidence of his arousal, Ellis hissed, "Yes, god, *please*."

His own cock throbbed at the desperation backing the plea, but Cinder wasn't ready to up the ante yet. Ellis would have to wait. In place of giving in to Ellis's desperate entreaty, Cinder scooted forward so he could reach the round globes of Ellis's ass.

He explored the smooth skin, relishing the muscled contours flexing beneath his touch. A single bead of sweat trickled down Ellis's stomach, diverting into the central crevice created by stark lines of muscle and sinew. Cinder yearned to follow in its path with his tongue, but instead placed a finger in his mouth to coat it with slippery wetness.

"Spread your legs farther apart, baby." Cinder made the command in a raspy whisper and was pleased when Ellis did as he'd been asked with continued keen cooperation. "That's right. Like that. Good boy."

When Ellis whimpered in clear appreciation of the encouragement, Cinder grinned and slipped his hand between Ellis's legs. He stroked a featherlight finger along the crack of Ellis's ass without pressing deeper, pairing the questioning touch with a gruff, "May I?"

Ellis tipped back his head and garbled out another desperate plea. "*Yes*. God, please. *Yes*."

That response sent Cinder's pulse racing at record-breaking speed, and without another moment's pause, his moistened digit found its goal. As soon as he touched the puckered flesh, a shudder ran through Ellis, and when he swirled his finger in a series of tiny, focused circles, Ellis's knees buckled. His eyes flew open, and his hands fell to rest on Cinder's shoulders for support. A frantic, reckless cry slipped past his lips as his fingers dug in for dear life.

"You okay?" Cinder paused his movement, placing his free hand on Ellis's hip to steady him. "I can stop. Just say the word."

"Fuck, no." Ellis snapped the words, a broken laugh following in their wake as he shook his head. A slew of half-formed sentences fell from his trembling lips. "Never felt anything… It's good. *Too* good. Want more, not less. *So good*."

Cinder stifled a chuckle as he set back to work. "Eyes closed. I don't want you to do anything but *feel*."

Ellis sucked his lower lip between his teeth and squeezed his eyes closed. When Cinder breached his opening, Ellis's fingertips dug into Cinder's shoulders, his hips rocking forward. And when Cinder's probing finger found that holiest of spots and curled to press against it, Ellis fell apart at the seams. A stream of curses slipped past his lips. His body shuddered and swayed, his mouth falling open and leg muscles quivering.

"Feel good, baby?" Cinder pressed a kiss to the inside of Ellis's trembling forearm. "Want me to keep going?"

Eyes flashing open, Ellis huffed out a breath and

blinked in dazed awe at Cinder, who offered a cocky smirk in response. Ellis swallowed and licked his lips before wheezing, "Feels *so good*. Think I could come without... without you even t-touching my... my..." His head fell back on a deep, rumbling groan when Cinder stroked that spot again. And again.

Cinder's lips curled even further until he was quite sure they resembled something worn by a supervillain about to destroy his prey. "Oh, sweetheart. I could make you come a hundred different ways if you'd let me." He moved his finger in a slow, deliberate circle, savoring Ellis's choked gasps. "This is only the beginning."

With a gentle tug, Cinder freed his finger, delighting in Ellis's grunt of dissatisfaction at the loss. "Lie on your back and drape one leg over the back of the couch." Cinder patted the cushion beside him, holding back a grin at Ellis's stumbling eagerness to comply. When he was positioned as Cinder had asked, with his head propped on the armrest and his legs splayed open, Cinder rewarded him with a single fingertip traced up the underside of his cock.

At the first breath of contact, Ellis whimpered, his dick throbbing in a plea for more. Instead of complying, Cinder kissed Ellis's ankle and stood. "Don't move a muscle. I'll be right back."

With that, he disappeared to his dressing room to retrieve a few necessary items. When he returned with his treasures in hand, he found Ellis exactly as he'd left him— gloriously spread, panting, and flushed with the need to be touched and teased. To be worshiped and indulged. But most importantly, the need for all those things to come from *him*. Cinder. *Henry*.

Ellis's Henry.

After kicking the door closed, Cinder returned to Ellis and set the condoms and lube on the coffee table beside them. He stroked a hand up the inside of Ellis's thigh, then stopped a hairsbreadth from his groin and grinned. "Lie back and relax, baby. I'm going to make you feel so fucking good."

Chapter Thirteen

enry settled between Ellis's legs, still fully clothed, and hungrily traced every inch of Ellis's naked body with those gorgeous hazel eyes. Again. For the umpteenth time. Worshipping him in a way Ellis had never experienced before. In a way he might never experience again.

Every experience Ellis had ever had with sex was quick, dirty, and almost always one-sided. It had never been like this. He'd never been the one receiving all the attention. Hell, in the past he was lucky to be noticed at all. The men he'd chosen to sleep with had demanded his mouth or ass to slake their needs and had rarely offered to return the favor.

He'd known he had a submissive personality. It was obvious in the way he related to people around him—even more so in the type of men he'd once picked to warm his sheets. But one too many bad experiences in that department had left him leading a life of voluntary celibacy.

Until Henry.

Henry was the first man Ellis had wanted to be with in over half a decade. He was also the first man who had ever asked for permission before touching him and kept checking in to be sure Ellis was on board with every shift in dynamics. He had the dominant personality Ellis had continuously sought in a lover, only without the asshole bits that broke his spirit and left him feeling mentally hollow and physically empty.

Rather than reminding him of those regrettable sexual experiences, Henry's tender commands and doting devotion left Ellis satisfied in a way he'd never been before. Fulfilled yet yearning for more.

Henry retrieved something from the pile of goodies he'd brought back from his dressing room before placing a gentle, protective hand over Ellis's hipbone. "I'm not pretending to know or to care what your sexual history has been, but I'll admit mine has been extensive." He held up a raspberry-flavored condom, his stare boring into Ellis's. "I'm going to use this today because I respect you, not because I don't trust you. Safety for us *both* always comes first, which is why I want us to get tested. Because I want to be exclusive, and I want the freedom to put my mouth on you. Everywhere. Whenever I want. Sound like a deal?"

Ellis gaped for only a moment before slamming his jaw closed so fast his teeth vibrated from the impact. Henry wanted to be exclusive. With Ellis. As in—

"Yes, that's my super unromantic way of asking you to go steady. Or whatever the hell you kids are calling it these days." Henry winked and kissed the inside of Ellis's knee. "Now, may I?" He ripped open the foil packet with his teeth and presented the berry-colored condom for Ellis's inspection. "I want you in my mouth when you blow."

A whimper slipped through Ellis's tightly clenched jaw, but he managed to squeak out a verbal agreement.

Henry's lips curled into a cocky smirk as he pinched the tip of the condom and rolled it down Ellis's length. Ellis had to bite his tongue to keep from screaming with repressed need and desire. No one had ever touched him like this, through a condom or not.

Such selflessness and consideration. Such painstaking care. And—another first—this flawless moment was being shared not between two people with mere physical attraction between them, but two men in a mutual *relationship*. A level of commitment and connection that stretched deeper than anything he'd experienced before.

The stupidest grin pulled at his lips, only growing wider when Henry caught it out of the corner of his eye and paused to arch a questioning brow. "Telling someone I want to make them come with my mouth doesn't usually inspire childish glee."

Shaking his head, Ellis laid a hand over Henry's. "It wasn't *that*. Although, that definitely, ah, yeah. No words."

"Mm-hmm." Henry laced his fingers with Ellis's, using his other hand to trace circles over the inside of Ellis's thigh. Moving closer and closer with every finished loop of his finger to the spot where he wanted him most. "Then what's the dopey grin for, if not in response to my promise of"—Henry finally reached his target and cupped Ellis's balls in the soft warmth of his palm—"*divine pleasure*."

A groan escaped Ellis's throat, but he clenched his jaw and tried to keep his focus on Henry, not the tingling jolts of yearning firing through his core. "Yeah, well, I suddenly have myself a *committed partner*. Apparently. Makes this whole thing... a whole new level."

Henry let loose a delightful laugh before stretching over Ellis's body to plant a deep, satisfying kiss on his lips. "More on that later, when I'm not about to blow your mind, but yes. You're mine, and I'm yours. Now, *eyes closed*. Don't make me blindfold you."

Electricity sparked over Ellis's skin, and he huffed out a breath, causing Henry to meet his gaze. Licking his lips, Ellis stretched his arms up and laced his fingers behind his head. Just as Henry had asked him to do while he was standing. "I have a bit of a one-track mind. If you want me to keep my eyes closed when there's so much I want to look at... Well, a blindfold might be necessary." Ellis winked when he caught the slight widening of Henry's eyes. "And if you don't want my hands getting in the way when there's so much I want to touch..." He shrugged and pressed his lips together. "You might want to do something about that too."

"*Have mercy.*" Henry closed his eyes for the briefest of moments, as if collecting himself, before boring his stare into Ellis's. "You're full of surprises today."

Ellis scraped his teeth over his bottom lip. "There's nothing wrong with a little light bondage between friends."

Henry narrowed one eye and casually took Ellis's balls in hand once more. He rolled them between his fingers and thumb with a gentle massaging motion that did nothing to quell the fire burning at Ellis's core. "I'll keep that in mind."

When Henry licked his lips and bent to take Ellis into the tight heat of his mouth, Ellis gasped. He struggled to keep his hips from thrusting toward that delicious warmth, focusing instead on the sensations as Henry chose to give them. Allowing Henry's lips and tongue and hands to guide his experience.

All too soon, that delicious pressure built at his core, signaling an imminent release. But he didn't want to come alone. "Henry. Stop. Please."

Doing as Ellis asked, Henry pulled away. His lips were swollen and his eyes dark and hungry. "You okay?"

"Better'n ever." Ellis pointed to Henry, indicating his fully clothed state with a swirl of his finger. "Except for all that. Need you naked. Need you inside me."

Henry growled low in his throat and lunged forward to take Ellis's mouth with feral possessiveness. When Ellis rocked his hips into Henry's, their kiss broke on a shared moan.

Grabbing his T-shirt by the hem, Henry yanked it

over his head and tossed it to the floor near Ellis's jeans. His pants and underwear followed in one quick, eager movement. Within seconds, he was back on Ellis, their bare bodies writhing together with shameless greed as their mouths crashed together in a gluttonous whirlwind of teeth and tongue and lips.

Ellis touched and tasted every inch of Henry that his insatiable hands and mouth could reach. He'd never felt so aware of his own body and yet somehow also hyper focused on someone else's. He wanted in a way he'd never wanted before. He needed in a way he never thought possible. "*Please.*"

It was all he could get out. One breathy, pleading word. But Henry understood without further explanation. He trailed kisses down Ellis's body as he reached for another condom and the bottle of lube. When he lifted to his knees to dress his cock with the rubber barrier, Ellis got his first good look at Henry's gorgeous body.

Throwing out a hand to stop Henry from rolling the condom on, Ellis sucked in a quivering breath and took his fill. Henry wasn't as heavily muscled as Ellis, but the hard work he put into his craft was evident by leanly sculpted muscles under soft, smooth skin. "You're breathtaking."

It was rare for Henry to show his bashful side, but a light dusting of pink highlighted his freckles. "That's a true compliment coming from someone as beautiful as you."

Ellis ran his hands up Henry's thighs. "I've never felt beautiful before, but damn if I don't when you look at me like that."

That secret, quiet smile Henry only ever shared with Ellis crept up his lips. "Then I'll have to remember exactly how I'm looking at you and make sure to do it all the time."

He bent to offer Ellis a soft, sweet kiss before rolling on the condom and squirting lube into his palm. Coating his fingers, he returned them to where it all began—with him inside Ellis, pressing on that spot Ellis had known existed but had never found. His gentle smile turning wicked, Henry spread the remaining lube on his dick, watching with delight as Ellis squirmed under his touch.

When he was finished prepping Ellis—with all the love and care Ellis had always wanted but had never received—Henry slipped Ellis's condom off and tossed it to the floor, then hooked his arms under Ellis's knees and locked their gazes. "Ready?"

"More than." Ellis cried out when Henry breached his opening, but it was with joy and pleasure rather than discomfort or pain. And when Henry's eyes drifted closed as he moved with the most tender, delightful rhythm, Ellis marveled at the sparks firing over his skin. Especially when Henry shifted his hips with expert precision, wrapped his hand around Ellis's bare cock, and with his very next thrust, nailed Ellis right where he needed it most. "*Holy fucking shit.*"

That's all it took. One stroke of Henry's dick against that bundle of nerves, paired with his warm grip, and Ellis saw stars. His whole body vibrated with the intensity of his orgasm, and the heavy rush of blood in his ears muted the joyful cry of Henry finding his own release only a few moments later.

They lay there together, sprawled awkwardly over the couch and twitching as aftershocks rocked through their systems, until Henry finally pushed to an elbow. Staring down at Ellis, he grinned. "That was *so* worth the wait."

With the goal of finding sustenance after they'd all but drained themselves to within an inch of life, Ellis and Henry slipped out the private employee side door to the theater. Henry took Ellis's hand, lifting it so he could brush a kiss over their joined knuckles. When their eyes met, he waggled his brows and tugged Ellis in for a kiss, whispering against his ear, "I can't wait to get you naked again," before pulling away.

Heat prickled at Ellis's cheeks, but as he struggled to formulate a proper response, his worst nightmare—in the shape of a gaggle of groupie fans who had somehow recognized country boy Henry outside of his goth-punk Cinder stage garb—swooped in to ruin the moment.

High-pitched shrieking and the unwelcome clawing of hands as the horde of adoring admirers closed in around them clouded Ellis's brain with a rush of panic and claustrophobia. But unlike last time, there were no burly bodyguards to keep the crowd at bay. Instead, they continued to press closer and scream louder until the remnants of Ellis's sanity slipped away.

It wasn't until he heard Henry's clear, controlled voice in his ear, ordering him to turn around and go back inside the theater, that Ellis snapped out of his comatose terror and found the will to seek safety. But when he shoved through the growing throng and fumbled his keycard from his pocket so he could open the door, Henry was nowhere to be seen. He hadn't followed Ellis, but instead remained trapped at the heart of the mob.

No way was Ellis going to let his own weakness and anxiety cause Henry to face that horror alone. He started back toward the chaos but was stopped in his tracks by AJ, the bodyguard who had rescued him the previous time. "Cinder wants you back inside. He's going to give out a few autographs and take a few selfies. Don't worry. Emmitt's with him. He'll be safe."

Ellis nodded blindly, allowing AJ's hulking form to guide him into the theater and deposit him into Henry's dressing room like a toddler in timeout. AJ pointed to the door handle as he backed out of the room. "Lock up behind me. Just in case. I'm gonna go play backup."

Again, Ellis merely offered a mechanical nod in response.

"Keep an eye on your phone. We might need to extract Cinder via vehicle. I'm sure he'll be in touch." With that, AJ exited the building and left Ellis slumped on the couch, reeling from yet another brush with the pandemonium that ruled Henry's life.

Ellis dropped his head back onto the cushion and stared up at the ceiling in self-defeat. He couldn't even handle a moment under the weight of fame-by-association. Could he and Henry really have a future together when he couldn't stomach the pressure of Henry's everyday existence? Would Henry want Ellis around if it meant an added burden for his security team, requiring them to whisk Ellis away at the first sign of trouble only to leave Henry with insufficient coverage in the event of an emergency?

Squeezing his eyes closed, Ellis mumbled a curse before pressing to his feet. Whatever he and Henry had planned for that evening, it was off the table now. He needed to do something to get his mind off this mess.

When Henry reached out, as Ellis had no doubt he would, Ellis would figure out how to respond. For now, he'd change into work clothes and let the job beat his body into submission. A pale replacement for an evening with Henry, but an apt punishment for his feeble vulnerability.

Chapter Fourteen

When Cinder's phone rang, he nearly dropped it in his fumbling hurry to answer. Hope fizzled in his chest when he saw it wasn't Ellis, and he frowned at the caller ID instead. But if there was anyone in the world who could make him feel better right now—save Ellis himself—it would be the woman on the other end of the phone. "Hey."

"Well, don't you sound like a ray of sunshine this morning," Kumiko chortled. "I take it you aren't a fan of the new celebrity couple name the fans chose. Personally, I think it's delightful."

Cinder pinched the bridge of his nose and resumed the pacing he'd been doing before Kumiko called. "What are you talking about? What name?"

Kumiko cackled, her voice muffling as she covered the microphone to speak to her wife. Cinder caught a few words but couldn't tell what was being said. Eventually, Lizbeth took control of the phone, laughter lacing her words. "Henry Cinderford, you and that sexy stagehand have the *best 'ship name ever*. You're on speaker so we can both hear your reaction, but I won the right to tell you, since you've somehow had your head buried in the sand. Are you ready?"

Sighing, Cinder motioned her on before remembering she couldn't see him and clicked his tongue in irritation. "Go ahead, Liz. Spit it out."

Lizbeth giggled and another whispered exchange occurred before she finally blurted out, "Cinderellis. Your couple name is *Cinder-freaking-Ellis*."

They emitted a joint ear-splitting squeal before Kumiko took control of the conversation again. "Tell me that isn't adorably perfect. It was meant to be."

Cinder paused a moment as the reality of the ridiculous tabloid nickname sank in.

Cinderellis.

Fuck.

As if things weren't complicated enough right now. Ellis wasn't going to be happy about this. Especially not considering his intense desire to keep everything *them* a secret. If they had an official 'ship name, it meant the press had figured out who Ellis was, which meant they might know things about him, like where he worked and where his family lived.

"*Shit.*" Cinder bolted for the garage, pausing only long enough to snag his wallet, keys, sunglasses, and a ball cap. "I've gotta go, babes."

"Wait, what? What's wrong?" Kumiko shifted from her laid-back off-hours voice to the clipped professional tone she used to manage the troops. "Where are you going?"

As he shifted his Jeep into reverse, Cinder hit the Bluetooth button on his dash to switch the call to hands-free mode and dumped his cell in the cupholder. "I have to check on Ellis. If they have his name, who knows what else they know about him. I need to make sure he's safe and handling the news okay."

Kumiko's voice tightened even further as it sounded over the speakers. "You've got Emmitt and AJ in tow, right?"

"Don't I always?" Cinder checked his rearview mirror to be sure he wasn't lying, and when he saw the familiar SUV trailing a car length behind, he tossed his faithful tail a wave. "I might have to take a rain check on dinner and drinks later. It'll depend on how things go with Ellis. I haven't heard from him since last night, so I'm a little worried."

After being escorted home to safety the night before, Cinder had reached out to Ellis to apologize for the unexpected mauling. Ellis had been understanding and insisted Cinder had no reason to feel bad or ask for forgiveness. However, rather than accepting Cinder's offer to pay for an Uber so they could continue their evening as planned, Ellis had begged off, stating he had a big project to work on and should really get to bed so he could get up early the next day.

Cinder had accepted the disappointing change of plans with as much grace as possible, but when he'd tried to contact Ellis several times that morning to no avail, his nerves had taken a hit.

Things with Ellis were going too well to let the frantic chaos of Cinder's fame get in the way. He refused to let that part of his life endanger the first real relationship he'd ever had. It didn't matter that they hadn't had a conversation about where things were going between them. That level of formality wasn't necessary after what they'd shared the previous evening.

"Be careful, boo." The frown was evident in Kumiko's voice. "Hopefully, Ellis slept late and hasn't even heard the news. Either way, let us know everything's okay, will you? We'll worry."

"Yeah, don't make us wait too long." Lizbeth's voice was faint and no longer on top of the mouthpiece. Her nervous pacing had likely set in—a habit they shared. "There are three of us holding our breath over here now. Don't make the poor kid turn blue."

Cinder spent another minute or two assuring them he would at least shoot over a text once he'd connected with Ellis, then hung up. He had reached the Strip by then and was stuck in standstill traffic, as per usual. By the time he pulled into the garage and parked near the Colosseum's private employee entrance, another twenty minutes had gone by and Ellis had failed to answer three more of Cinder's phone calls.

To say his nerves were shot would be an understatement. He hopped out of his Jeep, then paused only long enough to fill his security team in on his concerns before hauling ass into the theater.

Calling Ellis's name, Cinder headed straight for the old green room that acted as Ellis's makeshift bedroom. He knocked once, then pushed the door open without waiting for an answer. It was empty.

With his jaw clenched, Cinder shouted for Ellis again as he jogged toward the backstage area. Mercifully, Ellis's sweet voice carried from the rafters a few seconds before he came into view, standing on a metal support beam less than a foot wide. "Henry?"

Cinder's stomach performed a complicated somersault that managed to encompass the nauseating chill he associated with his childhood fear of heights combined with stark-naked relief. "Jesus, my dude. Shouldn't you have a spotter if you're gonna be that high off the ground?"

A chuckle echoed through the fly space as Ellis crouched so he'd be a whole three feet closer to Cinder before replying, "I've been doing this for over a decade now. I've got my safety gear. That's more than enough." He tilted his head when Cinder swiped at the cool sweat prickling at his brow. "What's wrong? Are you afraid of heights?"

Scoffing, Cinder shoved both hands into the front

pockets of his jeans. "Who, me? Course not." When Ellis flattened his lips to hide a smile, Cinder rolled his eyes and huffed out a dejected sigh. "Okay, yeah, guilty as charged. Never been a huge fan. Would you mind coming down? You're making me dizzy looking at you all the way up there."

Cinder waited with his eyes cast to a safe level as Ellis made his way to the ground. When his feet hit the cement with a quiet thud, Cinder glanced up and locked on to Ellis's crystal-blue irises. Before the smile of alleviated welcome could lift his lips, Cinder caught sight of the rest of Ellis's face and his own pinched into a concerned frown instead. "What the fuck? What happened? Jesus, are you okay?"

Ellis parried out of Cinder's reach when Cinder tried to touch his cheek, darting his gaze away to hide the worst of the damage. "It's nothing. I'm fine. I promise."

"That's not nothing." Cinder's voice came out barely above a whisper, the words further distorted by the tight clench of his jaw. "Who did this to you? Did you get attacked by fans or—"

Holding up a hand to halt Cinder's questions, Ellis shook his head. "It's not a big deal. Don't worry about it."

Taking a deep, steadying breath, Cinder cracked his knuckles to give himself a moment to cool down so his next words wouldn't come out laced with the fiery rage boiling his blood. "I'll get you a security team. This won't happen again."

When Ellis speared a hand into his blond locks and let his eyes flutter closed on a soft groan, Cinder took the opportunity to really assess the damage. Whoever had attacked Ellis was a lefty. His bottom lip was swollen and split on the right side with shadowed bruising around the corner of his mouth and jaw. A freshly scabbed-over laceration slashed through his right eyebrow and the beginnings of a shiner had his lids looking puffy and faintly purplish.

Dropping his hand and locking eyes with Cinder once more, Ellis furrowed his brow. "I don't need a security team. It wasn't anything like that."

"No?" Cinder crossed his arms and raised a single brow. "If it wasn't like that, then how *was* it?"

Heaving an exaggerated sigh, Ellis dropped his chin and focused his gaze on his hands as he fidgeted with one of the straps on his harness. "I got into a fight with my stepdad. It was a stupid family thing. Seriously, don't worry about it, okay?"

His stepdad did this to him? As in, the asshole audio engineer? Cinder scowled. "I hope you gave him as good as you got. What the hell were you two fighting about, anyway?"

Darting a quick glance at Cinder, Ellis shrugged. "Like I said, it was a family thing."

Pinching the bridge of his nose, Cinder sucked in a slow, calming breath. "I'm sorry for prying, but you had me worried when you didn't answer any of my calls. After last night, I was—"

"*Shit.*" Ellis patted at his pockets, then let his head fall back. "I must've left my phone on the charger by my bed. I'm sorry. The old man kinda surprised me early this morning. Threw me a bit outta whack."

No surprise there. Cinder's morning would've been thrown outta whack too if he'd woken up to a fist in the face. "Are you sure you're okay? Have you put any ice on that? The swelling looks pretty bad."

Ellis touched his fingertips to the corner of his mouth and winced. "Nah, I'm okay. I've got a lot of work to get done. If it's bothering me, I'll ice up later."

Cinder bit back a sigh. "Why don't you take a break? I can settle you on my dressing room couch and play nurse."

Pressing his lips together, Ellis shook his head. "I really don't have time. I already had a lot on my plate, then Ray dumped even more on it this morning."

"Is that what you fought about?"

It was wrong of him to keep pressing the subject, but something felt off. Ellis wasn't the type to get into a fist fight with someone. For any reason. Which meant whatever happened, it had likely been his asshole stepfather who initiated it. And Cinder was fairly certain he could knock down that bastard's door right now and not find a single hair out of place.

Ellis lifted a shoulder but kept his gaze averted. "It was more like my punishment for the thing we fought about." His cheeks pinked, and he squeezed his eyes closed. "Sorry, that came out wrong. Ray would never—"

"Yeah, he would. And he did." Cinder balled his hands into fists but schooled his voice to remain calm. "Does the theater know how much of a snake that man is? Maybe I should enlighten them."

Eyes flashing, Ellis locked his stare on Cinder, his head shaking furiously back and forth. "No. Please. Don't. You can't."

Cinder held up his hands, palms out in deference. "Hey, hey. Don't worry. I won't do anything you don't want me to do." A creeping sense of suspicion and dread itched up his spine, and his "something seriously ain't right" radar pinged off the charts. Until he got the truth out of Ellis, he wasn't leaving him alone.

A thought niggled its way into his brain, and he smiled. "I'm bored off my ass. Why don't you put me to work? There's no way I'm going up *there*"—Cinder pointed to the heavens—"but I've got a strong back and follow directions well."

Ellis frowned. "No way."

Laughing, Cinder clapped Ellis on the shoulder. "Come on, my dude. Four hands can do twice the work of two. Let's buckle down and get this shit done—together—then we can take the evening off. Together."

"This isn't your job, Henry. It's *mine*." Ellis rubbed

at the back of his neck. "I'd get fired if anyone found out I had *Cinder* slaving away on remedial grunt work behind the scenes. Plus, Ray would be pissed. I'm already in enough hot water with him. I don't need to make things worse."

"Well, it's a good thing no one's gonna find out, huh?" Cinder adjusted his baseball hat, so the bill faced backward, and rolled his shoulders. "I won't take no for an answer. Come on, babe. Put me to work. Use me." He winked and waggled his brows. "Trust me, I have every intention of repaying the favor later. As soon as I get you naked again, I plan to make *very* good use of you."

Ellis's eyes widened and his Adam's apple bobbed when he swallowed, slow and deliberate. "Ah, okay then." He cleared his throat and looked away, failing to hide the grin tugging at his lips. "Follow me."

Chapter Fifteen

Henry flopped onto the gray suede sectional with a dramatic and exaggerated groan. "My dude, I don't know how you bust that much ass on a regular basis. All the muscles in my body—including some I wasn't even aware existed—are screaming."

With a chuckle, Ellis joined Henry on the couch. He went into Henry's arms when he opened them in invitation and snuggled against his bare chest. After they'd arrived at Henry's house and taken their respective showers, they'd changed into lounging clothes, and Henry hadn't bothered putting on a shirt. Much to Ellis's delight.

"You get used to it." Ellis flattened a tentative palm over Henry's chest. "It's a different kind of exercise, that's all. I guarantee I'd die a million deaths if I had to run around the stage like you do, belting out songs at the top of my lungs while sweltering under those damn sauna lamps. It's endurance versus strength. And I've got slim to no endurance."

"And I've got slim to no strength." Henry squeezed

Ellis's bicep and tugged his lips into a sexy, crooked grin. "At least, nowhere near the pure brute strength you do. My god, watching you today about did me in. *Hubba, hubba.* Although..." He tapped his chin and hummed in thought. "I bet you have far more *endurance* than you think you do. I'd be willing to test that theory the next time we have a nice long stretch of freedom to play with."

Ellis bit back a moan and flexed his fingers into a momentary fist before once again splaying them over the solid warmth of Henry's chest. "That sounds..." He closed his eyes and allowed a series of images to dance across the back of his eyelids. Images of all the things he could imagine in that moment that Henry might do with a *long stretch of freedom.* Clearing his throat, Ellis opened his eyes and focused on a loose thread at the waistline of Henry's gray sweats to keep himself from falling any farther down that rabbit hole. "Yeah, that sounds like a definite plan."

Henry kicked his legs up to rest on the coffee table, crossing them at the ankle before guiding Ellis down so his head lay on Henry's lap. He carded his fingers through Ellis's hair, massaging them into his scalp until Ellis all but turned into a purring puddle.

"Did it ever frighten you? Being so high up there without a net to catch you if you fall?"

Ellis shook himself out of his pleasure haze and furrowed his brow as Henry's words worked into his brain. "I guess so. At the beginning. But I needed a job, and landing a gig as a stagehand at one of the most highly respected theaters on the Strip was one hell of an honor. Ray said it would all but guarantee me an eventual spot on an audio engineering team, which has always been the dream." Ellis's frown deepened. "I guess I thought I'd be there by now. At the very least, I thought I'd be doing mic wrangling duties rather than hiding away in the rafters. But that's showbiz for ya. Nothing's ever guaranteed. I'm just happy to have a job that still leaves the possibility open for a brighter future."

At least, he hoped the possibility was still there. After his run-in with Ray, Ellis couldn't even be sure he'd still have a job in a few days' time. Ray had been a special level of fuming mad when he'd woken Ellis out of a dead sleep that morning, ranting and raving about something that hadn't made a lick of sense in Ellis's barely awake, exhaustion-addled brain.

Until, of course, it had made *all* the sense.

Cinderellis. Quite the apropos 'ship name, wasn't it?

His and Henry's relationship fit the bill rather nicely, really. Cinder had been dubbed the new Prince of Pop and Ellis's bank account only went into the triple digits for twelve or so hours following the direct deposit of his salary before the biweekly check he sent to Ray cleared and he was back down to the pauper's pittance he survived on.

But it wasn't the cutesy nickname that had Ray so up in arms. He'd warned Ellis time and again not to involve himself with the talent, and here he was, not only involved, but *dating* an international superstar.

Ellis didn't kid himself. Not anymore, at least. Ray's motivations for keeping him away from the acts had always been selfish. He'd played it off as being some sort of safety mechanism to assure Ellis wouldn't put his job at risk. Making it seem like Ray was looking out for him, that he was protecting Ellis from embarrassing himself or putting the talent out by getting under their feet when he was nothing but a lowly stagehand.

Maybe that was true with some of the acts over the years. Maybe it had even started out as a real concern, back when Ray had put his neck on the line to help Ellis get the job. But now? Now it was Ray trying to keep Ellis under his thumb. Controlling him for the sake of controlling him and getting pissy when Ellis wasn't as easy to manipulate as he used to be.

Or so Ellis liked to believe. In all reality, nothing had

really changed. He still feared Ray in much the same way a child might fear the monster under their bed. He could pretend all he wanted that he'd stand up to Ray, and perhaps part of him had started to push that invisible boundary within the safety of his own mind, but actually confronting the beast was a different story.

Still, it meant *something* that Ellis had chosen to follow Henry home tonight despite his stepfather's clear admonitions, didn't it? In all the years Ellis had known the man, Ray Brunswick had never given him anything without a threat of violence or ruination attached, including the flimsy piece of paper essentially declaring Ellis as Ray's legal obligation in the event of Maggie's death. A horrifying happenstance Ray hadn't counted on when he'd decided to adopt Ellis as some idiotic means of control and self-ego stroking.

This situation was no different. If Ellis continued to see Henry, and Ray discovered he hadn't heeded his pointed warnings, there would be hell to pay. As much as Ellis wanted to believe he could be man enough to stand up and say *fuck you* to the outlandish threats still ringing in his ears, the fact remained that they petrified him, and he had no clue how to move forward. He didn't want to lose what he was discovering with Henry, but could their tentative relationship survive his cowardice?

Even at twenty-six years old, with an inch of height and twelve-plus hours a day of hard, muscle-building labor over Ray's aging physique, Ellis remained terrified and under the man's control.

Sensing Henry's gears turning and wanting to keep things from going down a path he'd rather not travel, Ellis pushed to an elbow and locked their gazes. They'd chatted in passing throughout the day, and Ellis had admitted to hearing about Cinderellis. He'd also let it slip that it *might* have been part of his argument with Ray, which had turned Henry quiet and introspective.

The last thing Ellis wanted was for Henry to start putting two and two together. If anyone looked close enough, it wouldn't be hard to see Ellis still hadn't outgrown the childhood fear of his stepfather's wrath. He'd rather Henry not make that unattractive connection.

"Speaking of being afraid of heights…" Ellis grinned when Henry rolled his eyes, as if he knew where Ellis was steering the conversation without needing to hear the rest of his sentence. "What? You asked me about my fear, now I'm asking you about yours."

"Mm-hmm." Henry scoffed and tossed Ellis a wink before shaking his head with faux dramatic sincerity. "Can't a guy hold on to a ridiculous childhood phobia for no good apparent reason without being razzed for it?"

Ellis opened his mouth to counter that statement before realization struck and his jaw slammed closed with a rattle of teeth.

Wasn't that, in essence, the same general sentiment he'd wrestled to conclusion in his own roundabout way only moments before? He had no good reason to continue fearing his stepfather, yet the dreaded reactions of others if they found out that fatal flaw almost caused him more anxiety than Ray himself.

Not quite the same as Henry's statement, but close enough to give Ellis pause. Maybe he wasn't as alone in this particular area as he'd first thought. If Henry Cinderford—teen prodigy turned international heartthrob, complete with a platinum and diamond studded career—could harbor an Achilles' heel lying dormant since his youth, then *anyone* could.

And if Henry had the guts to confront his demons, maybe Ellis could too.

"Have you ever tried facing down your phobia to see if you could overcome it?" Ellis cocked his head and smiled at Henry's skeptical smirk. "I hear the best cure for a fear of heights is going somewhere really high and proving to yourself that you can look down and survive to see the next day."

"So you're saying I won't be afraid of heights anymore if I have the balls to put myself in extreme danger and live to tell the tale?" Henry's smirk morphed into a scrunched-nose sneer, causing his freckles to stand out in stark contrast against the blanched skin. "No, thanks."

Ellis laughed, a bubble of relief lifting free of his chest. He felt somehow less powerless knowing he and Henry shared similar disinterest in dispelling the age-old beasts on their backs. Sometimes it was easier to live with fear than to challenge the devil to proverbial fisticuffs.

"Although—" Henry drew out the word, then paused, as if considering his next words carefully. "—with a little patience, and you by my side while I work through the choking fear, I'm pretty sure I could tackle about anything you threw at me."

Or maybe they *weren't* on the same page. If Henry was willing to toss away his personal demons with the right support and motivation, maybe it was time for Ellis to reassess his priorities.

He either learned to defy his fears and have a chance at something amazing with Henry, or he kept hiding under the covers in his mind and risked losing everything.

Not the hardest decision to make, but finding the will to carry through with it was something else entirely.

"Fair enough." Ellis settled back on Henry's lap, grinning when Henry attempted to stifle a yawn. There'd been promises of adventurous sex as Henry's payment for helping Ellis with his workload, but rest seemed a better option at this point. "What do you say we throw in the towel and get some sleep? It's been a long day."

A sleepy hum of agreement met Ellis's words as Henry continued the steady, rhythmic stroking of his fingers through Ellis's hair. "I like the stound of that. Of getting you into my bed and waking up with you still there."

Despite all the time they'd spent together over the past few weeks, there had always been an end to their evenings. A time where sleep was inevitable, and they'd say their reluctant goodbyes before returning to their own beds for the night. But tonight, that would change. Tonight, Ellis would slip into the comfort of a real bed, pull Henry into his arms, and drift off to dreamland without a care in the world.

Tomorrow—or the next day, depending on how long it took for Ray to discover his brazen behavior—he'd face whatever repercussions came with his decision to give the old man the proverbial middle finger. Until then, he'd enjoy the fruits of his poor life choices to their fullest.

Ellis groaned deep in his throat when the warm softness of Henry's massive California king enveloped him, hugging his body in ways no bed ever had before. Henry chuckled as he slipped under the covers beside him and ordered Alexa to turn off his bedroom lights.

When the room sank into darkness, Ellis closed his eyes and allowed the decadence to engulf him. The hard heat of Henry's body appeared at his side, his stubbled cheeks tickling Ellis's neck when he planted a row of whisper-soft kisses along his jaw.

"If I didn't know any better, I'd think you worked my ass to the bone so I wouldn't have the strength to demand you make good on my reward." Henry traced his tongue over Ellis's lower lip in tandem with the hand he ran up Ellis's thigh beneath the covers. "Fortunately for us both, I know that isn't the case."

Tingles skated over Ellis's skin, and he shivered despite the warmth of his surroundings. "You're tired, and it's late…"

"Mm-hmm, I am, and it is. However…" Henry's

wandering hand skipped over the area covered by Ellis's boxer briefs and followed the lines of his abdominal muscles instead. "I've wanted you in my bed for ages now. There's no way I'm giving up the chance to have my way with you now that you're finally here."

"Oh god." Ellis swallowed a moan when Henry pressed flush against his side, the evidence of his arousal hard and thick at Ellis's hip. "I'm game if you are."

Chuckling, Henry nuzzled Ellis's cheek before sealing their lips together for a kiss. It started out soft and gentle but grew heated and fervent as Ellis turned to face Henry, their hands touching and grappling for purchase, their bodies pressing close and begging for *more*.

"I need to touch you," Henry growled, his hips bucking against Ellis's.

Ellis whimpered and nodded against Henry's throat, all but drowning in his own desire and ravenous need for the man in his arms. "Yes, god, please."

In the blink of an eye, the world tilted on its axis as a hot, calloused palm wrapped around Ellis, sans any clothing in between. Two seconds later, the velvety steel of Henry's cock met Ellis's, and Henry gripped them together. He stroked their lengths in the tight heat of his fist, sending sparks of electricity firing from the end of every nerve in Ellis's body. His muscles tightened, and he latched onto Henry's shoulders in a desperate attempt to find grounding in the storm of sensation rocking him from the inside out.

"I'm not going to last long." Henry's voice was gravelly and hoarse, his breaths fanning over Ellis's throat in erratic, panting waves. "You feel too good."

"*Ngh.*" Ellis could do nothing but garble out nonsense, words failing him as blissful pressure built at his core. When Henry's shoulders bunched under Ellis's hands, followed by a strained cry and a blast of wet heat between them, Ellis's own release slammed through him with the force of a freight train barreling through a tunnel.

Gasping and clinging to Henry as reverberations of the pleasure they'd shared twitched and shuddered through their bodies, Ellis buried his face in Henry's hair and thanked everything good in the world for giving him the gift of this moment. If everything fell to shit tomorrow, at least he'd have the memory of Henry—lying satiated and serene in his arms—to keep him company in the fallout.

Chapter Sixteen

As the amber and pink hues of a Vegas sunrise peeked through the blinds, the radiant heat of the muted rays fell in bands over the comforter, and Cinder's eyes drifted open. He blinked up at the ceiling as his mind meandered toward consciousness.

After waking up in the same surroundings for over two months now—the longest stint he'd ever had in the same sleeping quarters, if he didn't count his tour bus, which he didn't—he was finally starting to get used to the luxury of the familiar. He relished the recognizable comfort of a bed he could call his own and the intimate ease of a space he knew and could navigate without thought.

But as his brain chugged into gear, something struck him as different. Not wrong, just not the same as usual. He went to lift a hand to rub the sleep from his eyes but found his arm trapped by an unexpected weight. Before he could turn to assess the source of his encumbrance, enough awareness seeped into his mind to bring back memories of how he'd fallen asleep the night before.

Wrapped in the arms of Ellis Tremaine.

A smile crept up his cheeks as he rolled over to pull Ellis against his chest. Snuffling in his sleep, Ellis came willingly. He threaded a leg between Cinder's and circled an arm around Cinder's waist to anchor their bodies together. Smile stretching into a grin, Cinder brushed a kiss over the whorl of hair at Ellis's crown as he reveled in the beauty of waking to such a cozy, content moment.

This was what he'd been missing all these years. Every time he'd pushed another nameless partner from his bed in the wee hours of the morning—choosing to sleep alone after sharing a romp in the sheets rather than waiting to see where the morning might take them—he'd given up another chance at finding the one thing he'd needed most.

Comfort. Stability. A rock to cling to in the stormy seas of life.

A home.

Because that's what this was. This moment with Ellis in his arms, sated by memories of a day spent working side by side and an evening shared without the typical pomp and circumstance others required, it was the *home* he'd been searching for all his life. Just as his parents had always tried to tell him, but he'd never understood.

Home wasn't a physical space. It wasn't something you could find in a brick-and-mortar structure or by tying yourself to a single place. Home was a feeling. An emotion. A sense of well-being and security. Of being cared for and wanting to—no, *needing* to—care for another.

In its simplest form, home was love. And as Cinder clung to Ellis's sweet warmth, he knew *love* was where his heart was headed. Maybe he hadn't quite fallen that far yet, but it was coming for him, and he was ready to take the plunge when it did.

Sleep stole Cinder away again and when he awoke a second time, it was to Ellis leaning over him, planting a kiss on his temple. He was fully dressed and smelled of minty toothpaste. "Shh, no need to get up. I just wanted to say goodbye."

"What?" Cinder rubbed a knuckle into one eye as he squinted in confusion at the bedside clock. It was still early, only a little after seven. "Where are you going?"

Ellis chuckled and sank a hip onto the edge of the bed beside Cinder. "I've still got a lot of work to finish up before show prep starts for tomorrow. And no"—he put a finger to Cinder's lips before a protest could spill from them—"you are *not* joining me today. You deserve a day of rest before the next stretch of performances. Plus, you've already saved my ass. I can easily finish what's left on my own." He lifted his lips in a crooked half smile and brushed Cinder's bangs from his forehead. "In fact, if you're up for it, I'd like to take you on a date with all my free time this evening."

A tiny chill vibrated up Cinder's spine and his brows popped. "A date? Are you sure?"

After that disastrous run-in with the paparazzi and fans at the Cabo Wabo Cantina during their first and last attempt at a real date, Ellis had been as anti-public with their time together as a people-pleasing personality type could get. If Cinder hadn't learned to read him early in their relationship, he might've steamrolled Ellis into doing a whole slew of things he didn't want to do. Thankfully, Ellis's tells were easy enough to catch for anyone who took the time to look.

"Yes, I'm sure." Ellis rubbed his earlobe as his gaze fell from Cinder's. "I'm sorry I've been such a pain about doing things with you in public. It isn't about you or about us as a couple. I'm just used to living under the radar as much as possible. Getting noticed can be..." He shrugged but kept his eyes lowered. "It's complicated."

Cinder pushed to an elbow. "I understand. Or, as much as it's possible to understand when I grew up the way I did. But even for me, the crowds and attention can get overwhelming. I don't blame you for wanting to maintain a lower-key existence. I hate that being with me means that might be an impossibility at times, but I hope you know I'll never let anyone hurt you. I've already talked to Kumiko, and she's arranging a security team for you. It isn't the answer to all the evils that come with having a famous boyfriend, but it'll go a long way to making it more tolerable."

Curling his lips in, Ellis scowled. "A security team? You do *not* need to do that. I'm fine. No one comes after me unless I'm with you, and you've got that covered."

Suppressing the urge to stroke a finger over the purple bruises evident even in the waning light as the sun traveled over the house and no longer shone directly through the blinds, Cinder sighed. It was true that Ellis had only encountered fan and media mobs while in Cinder's presence thus far, but as soon as he became a recognizable face, that would change.

And if having a constant security presence deterred a certain asshole audio engineer from using Cinder's lover as a punching bag, all the more reason to make it happen. Sooner rather than later.

"It's already settled. They'll stay out of your way. Unless you're looking for them, you won't even notice they're there." Cinder gave Ellis's knee a reassuring squeeze. "In the meantime, you're going to let one of my guys take you back to the theater and make sure you get inside safe and sound. No arguments."

Ellis rolled his eyes but melted into Cinder's arms when he pulled him back into bed for a real kiss goodbye. Bad morning breath and all.

When Cinder arrived at the theater to pick Ellis up for their date later that evening, he was thrilled to find him waiting by the private employee entrance with a single red rose in hand. Dressed to impress in a pair of ass-hugging dark-wash jeans and a pale yellow short-sleeved button-down that was damn near painted onto his muscles, Ellis offered his patented shy smile as he held out the flower.

"I know it's cliché, but there was a vendor selling them outside the theater when AJ dropped me off this morning, and I couldn't resist." Ellis shrugged but his smile pulled into a grin when Cinder took the rose and ran its soft petals over his lips. "You look great, by the way."

Ellis had refused to give Cinder anything to go by for his secretive plans other than "Dress casual and comfortable." Considering Ellis appeared comfortable but hardly casual, Cinder was grateful he'd chosen to step up his game a bit. He'd donned a pair of tapered khaki shorts with a fitted black polo shirt. He'd even opted for a black cotton twill fedora in place of his typical ball cap disguise.

"You clean up pretty nice yourself, stud." Cinder winked. "So you gonna tell me where we're going now, or does the suspense continue until we get there?"

With a small chuckle, Ellis threaded his arm through Cinder's. "That depends."

"On?" Cinder cast a glance at Ellis as he guided them through the building toward the side door entrance. The same door they'd run into the paparazzi nightmare only a few days prior.

"On whether you trust me or not." They exited the door, and Ellis pointed to the curb where Emmitt and AJ sat waiting for them in the oversized black SUV. "I shored things up with AJ this morning, but he said you'd have to agree to be 'led blindly' as it isn't in their job description to keep things like the destination they're taking you to a secret."

As they slipped into the back of the vehicle, Cinder gave Ellis's hand a squeeze and lifted his voice to be heard up front. "Take us wherever Ellis told you to go. I don't want to know where it is until we get there."

"Aye, aye, boss." Emmitt saluted through the rear-view mirror, then pulled into traffic.

"I guess that means you trust me, eh?" A slight blush touched Ellis's cheeks when he met Cinder's stare. "That's going to prove to be either a really good thing or a really bad thing once you find out what I've got planned."

Cinder took Ellis's hand, threading their fingers together and offering a squeeze of encouragement. "I trust you, babe. No matter what you've got up your sleeve, I know I'm going to love it."

Ellis pressed his lips together and angled a playful, disbelieving glance Cinder's way. "I'm not so sure you will at first, but hopefully it'll grow on you. Eventually."

Narrowing his eyes, Cinder tugged Ellis closer so he could whisper into his ear. "There's only one thing I can think of that's going to grow on me tonight, and there's no doubt in my mind I'm going to love every minute of it."

A snort of laughter escaped Ellis as he rolled his eyes with mock exasperation. "Men. We're all the same, aren't we?" He leaned down so his next statement could be as clandestine as Cinder's. "While that is *definitely* in the cards for after, what I've got in mind to start the evening will probably do more to shrivel than grow that particular area of your anatomy. At least temporarily."

Frowning, Cinder pulled away to get a good look at the satisfied mirth dancing in Ellis's eyes. "Are we going for a cold swim?"

Before Ellis could confirm or deny, they stopped on an unfamiliar street in a part of the city Cinder had never been. He craned his neck to get a better view, but Ellis tugged him out of the car before he saw anything other than the standard Vegas fare—an excess of flashing lights and bright bawdy decorations. "Where are we?"

"Downtown Vegas, baby." Ellis opened his arms to encompass the sights and sounds around them. "Welcome to your first taste of the Fremont Street Experience."

Downtown Vegas. Cinder had read a little about the history of Las Vegas once and remembered Downtown Vegas being the original location of the area known today as the Strip, a gambling district with lavishly decorated hotel casinos and big-name entertainment. It was the side of Vegas still to this day associated with the old timey mob scene and held a wealth of history side-by-side with more modern attractions, like a performing arts center, various museums, and a recently built expo center.

But most intriguing of all was the Viva Vision Light Show, something Cinder had heard about time and again from anyone and everyone who had made tourist spot suggestions for his time in the infamous city. He hadn't bothered looking into it yet—especially after settling into the hermit groove with Ellis—but a sudden rush of excitement had him grinning and gripping Ellis's arm. "We haven't missed the light show, have we?"

Returning Cinder's grin with a big, dopey, adorable one of his own, Ellis shook his head. "Nope, it goes off at the top of every hour after nightfall."

Laughing like a child set free in a candy store, Cinder pulled Ellis toward the pedestrian mall that connected most of downtown's hotels and casinos. It was also the location of the light show, which was displayed on a ninety-foot-high barrel vault canopy that stretched four or five city blocks.

As they wandered down Fremont Street, hand in hand, they took turns pointing out various sights and sounds, including iconic hotel casinos such as the Golden Nugget, Golden Gate, Four Queens, and Binion's. When Cinder spotted Vegas Vic, the oversized neon cowboy that talked and waved at passersby from his spot over what used to be the Pioneer Club but was now a souvenir shop, he all but melted with glee. "We have to get a selfie."

With a chuffed laugh of agreement, Ellis posed with Cinder, grinning and flashing a thumbs-up beside Cinder's "hang loose" shaka sign—the pinky and thumb salute.

They continued their journey by exploring the souvenir shop, popping into each of the casinos to play a slot or two, and making sure to be in a prime location to view the next light show. Cinder nearly lost it when one of his own songs accompanied a fascinating display of colorful graphics as they danced across the mammoth screen. "Must've been one of the umpteen releases my agent has me sign on the regular. I had no clue I was part of this. Pretty amazing."

Ellis wrapped his arms around Cinder from behind, resting his chin on the top of his head. "It's one of the main reasons I wanted you to see it. I figured you knew."

Shaking his head, Cinder relaxed against Ellis's firm warmth and sighed with a level of contentment he hadn't experienced in a public setting in, quite possibly, ever. Everything with Ellis somehow felt both brand-new and as comfortable as a well-worn pair of sweats all at the same time. It was like magic. A magic he had no intention of giving up.

"There's one more thing I want you to see before we grab dinner." Ellis pulled away and took Cinder's hand. He guided him through the heavy throng of tourists until they reached the end of the canopied area. Casting Cinder a sidelong glance, Ellis pointed at a gaudy-looking building made to appear like a slot machine and boasting SlotZilla on its front. "Do you know what that is?"

Scrunching his nose, Cinder shook his head. That attraction hadn't been in his research. At least, not that he could remember. "Nope, doesn't ring a bell."

Nodding, Ellis turned to face Cinder. "There is absolutely no pressure to do anything—tonight or ever—but I thought I'd introduce it to you as an option. Something to consider." He tilted his head, a serious mask replacing the easygoing countenance he'd rocked all evening. "You've seen all the people zip-lining under the canopy, right?"

Had he ever. Cinder had marveled more than once at the balls it must take for those daredevils to harness up and fly over the crowds like that. "Sure."

"Well, SlotZilla over there is the origin point of the zip lines. I thought, if or when you might decide to face your fear of heights like we talked about last night, this might be a fun and unique way to do so. And I could fly down right at your side."

Cinder blinked as, sure enough, four people emerged from the topmost level of SlotZilla, harnessed to a zip line in the Superman position—face down and *soaring*. His stomach did an immediate about-face turn before sinking to his toes.

Could he really do that? Did he have the cojones to attach himself to a flimsy wire and catapult toward the earth?

Glancing at Ellis, who offered a tentative half smile and squeezed Cinder's hand in quiet encouragement, Cinder nodded to himself. He *could* do it. He'd meant what he'd said the night before. With Ellis at his side, he believed he could do *anything*. "Let's do it."

With a slight raise of his brow, Ellis licked his lips and swallowed. "Ah, I wasn't suggesting we do it right now. I meant it when I said there was no pressure. I just wanted you to know this was here so you could file it away and think about it for future consideration."

Insides settling with the jolt of confidence and certainty bolstering his resolve, Cinder shook his head. "Nope, I'm ready. I meant what I said too. If you come with me, I could face a mountain. This is nothing."

Ellis ran a hand over the buttons of his shirt and rolled his shoulders back, as if giving himself time to process Cinder's declaration. Eventually, he pressed his lips into a thin line and nodded. "Okay. I mean, I'm all aboard if you are, and we can always turn back if you change your mind." He tipped his chin toward the towering slot machine. "There are two options. We can fly seated, which is a two-block line that only reaches seven stories high, or we can fly superhero style facing the ground, which is five blocks long and peaks at eleven stories."

Scoffing, Cinder marched toward the building, hauling Ellis in his wake. "Go big or go home, my dude. Let's Superman this bitch."

Chapter Seventeen

Watching the normally reserved Henry bounce around like a giddy, human-shaped ping-pong ball was quite possibly the highlight of Ellis's year. Not only had they made it down the zip line unscathed, but they'd gone twice more before Henry would even consider breaking for dinner.

Thankfully, by the time they'd finished a decadent meal—on Henry, despite Ellis doing everything in his power to talk Henry out of his insistence on paying—the initial excitement had waned enough that Henry agreed to call it three and done. For tonight, at least.

As they clambered into the SUV with the full intention of heading back to Henry's to wind down from their adventure with a snuggle on the couch and a good movie, Henry's cell chirped in his pocket. He dug it out and grinned when he saw whoever it was texting him. "Mind if I make a quick call? I gotta tell Kumi I essentially leapt off an eleven-story-high building. *Three* times. She'll never believe it."

Waving him on with a satisfied smirk, Ellis sat back

to enjoy the scenery as they weaved through the city. He jumped when Henry smacked him on the shoulder and indicated the phone he held away from his ear; the mouthpiece covered by his palm.

In a stage whisper, he asked, "Do you mind if we make a quick pit stop at Kumiko and Lizbeth's? They offered us a nightcap in exchange for finally getting to meet the man I, and I quote, 'can't shut up about.'" He rolled his eyes skyward, then offered a shit-eating grin. "I mean, they aren't lying. You do seem to come up an awful lot in conversation lately."

Ellis's cheeks turned molten, and he slid lower in the seat, as if the supple leather could swallow him whole if he made himself small enough. But if Henry's closest friends wanted to meet him, he couldn't say no, and now seemed as good a time as any. "Yeah, that's fine."

Henry narrowed one eye and mouthed, "You sure?"

Forcing as genuine of a smile as he could, Ellis nodded. "Of course."

After studying Ellis with a skeptical eye, Henry pursed his lips and returned to his phone conversation. "We'll stop by but won't be staying long. I've promised my man an evening stretched out on the couch under a fluffy blanket. He has an early morning, and we have important things to get up to before I tuck him into bed beside me."

The heat at Ellis's cheeks bled over his entire face, even spreading its mortifying tendrils to the skin of his scalp and throat. He buried his face in his hands and groaned.

Henry signed off his call, directed Emmitt to make a detour to his friends' house, then snaked an arm around Ellis's waist and pulled him close. "I'm sorry if I embarrassed you, but once you meet these ladies, you'll realize what I said was tame at best. They've already got us swinging by the chandelier and having hot monkey sex in their mind's eye. Alluding to a little below-the-belt action won't shock or scandalize their couth sensibilities because the Matsura-Hodges duo doesn't have any."

From the front seat, AJ covered a laugh with a very unconvincing cough, and Emmitt pressed his lips together as if holding his own laughter in. With a resigned sigh, Ellis tossed Henry a pinched frown. "Hot monkey sex?"

"Yes, hot monkey sex. Ask these two." Henry motioned between Emmitt and AJ, who shared a guilty look before returning to their standard stoic expressions. "Their inability to keep their giggles to themselves should say it all, but Kumiko and Lizbeth—*especially* Lizbeth—are self-appointed Lecherous Lesbians. I'm not sure it's possible to live up to the epic greatness they've attributed to my sex life in those raunchy little brains of theirs. So just, ya know... Don't take anything they say too seriously."

When the slightest blush colored Henry's cheeks and he averted his gaze, Ellis narrowed his eyes and poked him in the chest. "That sounds like a guilty preface to me. Please don't tell me you're worried about your friends calling out your prior sexual adventures. I'm well aware you have a past slightly more *colorful* than my own. That doesn't bother me. We all have a history."

This time, AJ didn't even try to cover his snort of laughter. Henry shot him a glare and fished a balled-up receipt out of his pocket to toss over the seat in a show of childish defiance. "Keep your opinions to yourself, my dude."

Ellis nuzzled into Henry's neck. To regain some semblance of privacy, he lowered his voice and spoke against Henry's ear. "You made us appointments to get tested. We're being safe in the meantime. That's all that matters. Don't let what others think affect what we have."

"*Fuck*, I..." Henry bit his lip and shook his head, as if shaking away the thought he'd almost spoken aloud. "You're too good to me."

They pulled up outside what Ray had always condescendingly called a McMansion in a sprawling desert housing development. It was a bit cookie cutter, yes, but it was leaps and bounds nicer than the Boulder City home Ellis slaved to the bone to finance and maintain all in the name of Ray's comfort and his own emotional preservation.

When Henry knocked on the door a few minutes later, it was opened almost immediately by a tiny sprite of a woman with her auburn curls piled on top of her head in a messy bun. She closed her light gray eyes with an exasperated groan and clutched on to Henry's wrist. "Tell me you're sober. My wife is staring down the bottom of wine bottle number *two* for the evening. I'm about to crawl up the walls."

As if just realizing Ellis stood a step behind Henry, she craned her neck around his shoulder. Her brows popped wide as she tugged Henry in the door and shoved him into the depths of her home before locking a Cheshire-cat grin on Ellis. "Well, hello there, stud muffin. You must be He Who Makes Cin Turn to Mush himself. I'm Lizbeth."

She held out a hand, and they shook hello. Ellis liked her already. "Nice to meet you. Name's Ellis if you're looking for something a bit shorter to call me, although I'm okay with that extended moniker too."

Lizbeth tipped her head back on a cackle. When Henry tried to speak, she elbowed him in the gut, then pointed in the direction she'd already attempted to shove him in once. "Drunky is thataway. You're on duty now. Baby-on-board and I deserve a break." Henry squinted his gaze, but Lizbeth snapped her fingers and pointed once again down the hall. "Go. Don't worry about us. I'll take good care of your boy. Ellis and I are going to get acquainted somewhere far, far away from the shitstorm you inherited. Good luck, rock star. You're gonna need it."

With that, Lizbeth hooked an arm through Ellis's, hip bumped the door closed, and guided him in the opposite direction from the way she'd aimed Henry.

Ellis peered over his shoulder and snickered at the

sight of Henry standing in the foyer exactly as they'd left him, a bemused expression contorting his features into an adorably beleaguered mask.

Lizbeth led them into a comfortable sitting area decorated in what could only be called desert chic. The walls and ceiling were cream stucco, but the floor was a copper-toned stone tile with weathered wood moldings. The L-shaped couch and single armchair were a teal twill fabric with gold, white, and salmon accent pillows. Several cacti in planters dotted the space and red clay pottery in various shapes and sizes were spotlighted on the stone hearth.

She pulled him onto the couch beside her and brushed the back of her hand over her forehead. "Being married is a chore. Don't ever do it. Unless it's to Cinder, of course. That boy may be a stubborn ox, but he's got a heart of gold. Although"—she narrowed her gaze, trailing it up and down Ellis in an overt and critical assessment—"you'll have to pass muster before we'll permit you to have his hand. We protect what's ours. Consider yourself warned."

"Noted." Ellis rubbed at the back of his neck but relaxed a fraction when Lizbeth's expression softened.

"Any who." Lizbeth kicked her feet up on the gold and marble coffee table and laid a protective hand over her baby bump. "We've certainly heard a lot about you lately. Do you have anything to say for yourself, or should we take Cin's glowing accolades as info enough and move on to the interrogation portion of this little chat?"

"Ah…"

Lizbeth snorted and bumped Ellis's shoulder with her own. "I'm kidding. Cin hasn't given me any reason to doubt your worth, and he's a big boy. However, I meant it when I said we protect what's ours. So if you're thinking of breaking his heart, I suggest you put at least a zip code or two between Kumi and me before you do, capisce?"

Ellis almost busted out laughing until he realized Lizbeth was being stone-cold serious. He coughed to cover the almost-mistake and rubbed his sweaty palms over his jean-clad thighs. "I can't promise how things will turn out between us, because I'm not blessed with future sight. However, I *can* promise to treat Henry with the respect, devotion, and care he deserves."

Her jaw dropped and her eyes welled-up with a filmy layer of tears. "Ohmygod, did you call him *Henry*?" She fanned herself and sniffled. "Damn hormones. I'm not usually a crier, but seriously. That might be the cutest damn thing I've ever heard."

Frowning, Ellis tried to think back on his conversation with Henry when he'd learned his true identity. Henry had agreed to let Ellis continue calling him by the name he'd known him by up until that point, but had he mentioned anything about keeping that between them? Had Ellis just royally fucked up?

"What did I say? Why are you so pale all of a sudden?" Lizbeth sat forward, her eyes wide. "It looks like someone hooked a Shop-Vac to your circulatory system and drained you dry."

Before Ellis could think of something to say other than silently flapping his lips like a fish out of water, a loud crash echoed from the hallway, followed by a high-pitched squeal, a shout from Henry, and then a roaring, drunken cackle.

Lizbeth rolled her eyes and levered off the couch belly first, one hand supporting her back as she padded toward the sound of chaos. "Kumiko Matsura-Hodges, what the hell are you doing?"

Henry stumbled into the room, looking frazzled and harried. He flopped onto the couch beside Ellis and curled into him. "Hold me. I think she broke me."

Swallowing to coat his dry throat, Ellis circled an arm around Henry's shoulders as he nuzzled into Ellis's neck. "What happened out there?"

"Damn woman has lost her mind." Henry shook

his head, planting a line of kisses up the column of Ellis's throat. "One minute we're having a perfectly bizarre conversation that I couldn't repeat or make sense of if I tried, the next she's barreling down the hallway in search of… Raisinets? I think?"

"Raisinets?" Ellis scrunched his nose. "As in, the candy?"

"Hell if I know. I couldn't make a lick of sense out of anything she said. I kept having to pry her hands off the carving knife because I *think* she was trying to demonstrate how to pop the cork off a wine bottle with it. Which, I don't think you can do. There might be something about doing that with a champagne bottle, but those corks are different, and I…" Henry's rambling petered out with a muffled groan as he buried his face in Ellis's shoulder. "She totally killed my high off being high, man. Can we go home?"

Lizbeth entered the room then with a tall, slender, and gorgeous Japanese woman leaning heavily on her slim shoulders. She shot a pointed glare at Henry as she and her drunken charge fell in a heap onto the sofa, practically landing on top of Henry. He skittered out of the way and wound up in Ellis's lap.

"*He* wouldn't… lemme…" Kumiko squinted an angry eye at Henry, her finger pointing with wobbly focus in his general direction. "Wanna to jus' open…"

"This is the last time I'm leaving you in charge. Did you let her have *more*?" Lizbeth kicked Henry in the shin as she attempted to keep Kumiko propped up beside her. He cried out and placed a hand over the injured spot, but she bobbled her head in response, bulging her eyes in exasperation. "That was deserved, my friend. I'm the one that's going to have to clean up her vomit at 3:00 a.m., not you."

"Drinkin' fer three, bay-bee." Kumiko's slurred words were broken by a hiccup as she placed a hand over Lizbeth's stomach and giggled. "Muh girls."

Henry perked up at that. "Did you find out the sex?

Is it a girl?"

Casting a warm smile at Kumiko, filled with more love than Ellis could ever hope to illicit from another, Lizbeth nodded and covered her wife's hand atop her baby bump. "Yep. We're having a little girl. Found out today, which is why Kumi has damn near drank our wine cellar dry."

"Drinkin' fer you." Kumiko hummed, dropping her head to Lizbeth's shoulder.

"Yes, love, I know." Lizbeth stroked a gentle hand down Kumiko's sleek black hair, then shifted her attention to Henry and Ellis. "She thought it would be cute to celebratory drink for all three of us. You can see how well that turned out."

Henry scoffed as he rubbed at his shin. "Yeah, not well at all. She's gonna get an earful as soon as she's far enough free of tomorrow's epic hangover to grasp the words coming out of my mouth."

A loud snore rang through the room and Lizbeth sighed. "Well, looks like she's finally down for the count. Would you gents be willing to help a preggo lady out and carry this deadweight to bed?"

Henry bounced off Ellis's lap and pointed square at his chest. "You're the muscle in this relationship. I can still barely move after the workout you put me through yesterday. I'll navigate to the bedroom if you carry her ass there."

Lizbeth's eyes twinkled with mischievous delight. "I can only imagine what kind of *workout* you boys were getting up to—"

"Nope, not going there, Liz." Henry held up a hand and shook his head. He locked gazes with Ellis and motioned to Kumiko's slumped form with a questioning chin tilt. When Ellis gave a nod of agreement, Henry waited for him to scoop Kumiko into his arms, then led the way to their bedroom.

They deposited Kumiko in bed, then left Lizbeth

there to tuck her in. Henry urged Ellis toward the front door. "Come on, let's get the hell outta here while Liz is otherwise occupied."

Feeling more than a little overwhelmed after the whirlwind of the past half hour, Ellis gladly followed Henry out the door. As they piled into the SUV and headed for Henry's, Ellis closed his eyes and let his head fall against the back of the seat.

Apparently, being part of Henry's life came with more than the pandemonium associated with his rabid fan-base and eager media vultures. It also came with a circle of friends who loved and adored Henry in a way Ellis had never experienced before.

He was grateful for their presence in Henry's life, because he deserved that kind of devotion and support, but Ellis couldn't help the twinge of jealousy bubbling under the surface. Even if Henry wanted Ellis in his life, would his closest friends accept him?

As if he could read Ellis's mind, Henry placed a palm against Ellis's cheek and guided their gazes together. "I'm sorry for bringing you to meet them tonight. Wasn't the best timing. I'm sure Lizbeth was a bit out of sorts after dealing with Kumi's sloppy drunk ass all evening, so ignore anything she may have said that has you looking so forlorn, okay? They're great gals, but the Matsura-Hodges household was a hot ass mess this evening. We'll do a redo when Kumiko has her wits about her, and Lizbeth isn't gnashing her teeth in wifely frustration."

Ellis welcomed Henry's soft lips and the promise of not only a pleasant evening to come, but of unconditional acceptance and steadfast adoration. "Can I ask you a question?"

"Of course." Henry traced a thumb over Ellis's jaw, undoubtedly marking the spot still bruised by Ray's fists. "Anything."

"Did I screw up by calling you Henry in front of

Lizbeth?"

Henry drew back his chin, pinching his face in confusion for the briefest of moments before a wide grin stretched his lips. "Oh, I bet she liked that, didn't she?" He chuckled and shook his head. "Not at all, babe. Henry's my name, and it's what you call me. Has Lizbeth razzed me for having such an uncool given name when I'm supposed to be some 'trendsetting' pop star? Absolutely. But I love that you call me Henry, and I'm not ashamed by it one bit. At least, not when it's coming from you. However, I've threatened pretty much everyone else with life-altering limb breakage if they so much as utter the name. Consider it further proof of how special you really are."

When Henry winked and drew Ellis back in for another deep, delicious kiss, all the weight of worry slipped free of Ellis's shoulders. Henry knew how to make him feel special in a way no one ever had before. And tonight, Ellis would do everything he could to make sure Henry understood how *mutual* that feeling was.

Chapter Eighteen

When they finally got home after what had turned out to be a far more eventful evening than expected, Cinder barely got the front door closed before Ellis was on him. Those soft, sweet lips crushed over Cinder's, and that hard, beautiful body pinned him against the wall.

Never one to turn down anything Ellis had to offer—especially after he'd admitted to his discomfort with taking control—Cinder sank into his touch. He dropped his head back and allowed Ellis to feast at his throat, nibbling and kissing his way from Cinder's jaw to the hollow of his collarbone, a place he'd only recently discovered to be an indelible erotic zone.

On the tail end of a moan, Cinder gripped Ellis's biceps. "If you're not careful, I might wind up taking advantage of you. I'd planned to let you go to sleep after such a long, action-packed evening, but—"

"What if *I* want to take advantage of *you* for a change?"

Ellis's gruff voice blew over Cinder's ear, sending every last trace of his sanity packing up and heading south. When his knees gave out as his head swirled with dizzying and dirty thoughts, Ellis caught him by slipping his knee between Cinder's legs. The feel of that work-hewn muscle flexing against his growing erection was enough to draw a feral growl up Cinder's throat. "I'm all yours, baby."

With a gravelly laugh, Ellis pressed closer still, until he'd trapped Cinder against a literal rock and a hard place—Ellis's rock-solid body at his front and the hard inflexibility of the wall at his back.

"Thank you for making tonight so completely perfect, and for making me feel so special. Always." Ellis nipped at Cinder's earlobe. "Now, I want to make *you* feel special. Will you let me?"

Ellis rolled his hips and sent Cinder's thoughts spiraling into the gutter. He forced a façade of coherence to the forefront with what little lucidity remained in his upstairs brain. "I always feel special around you. And shouldn't I be the one thanking *you* for the utter flawlessness of this evening? After all, you were the one who surprised me with the most thoughtful, brilliant date I've ever—*Ngh*."

Chuckling, Ellis traced his tongue over Cinder's collarbone again before sucking gently at the sensitive skin. Rather than stopping to allow Cinder a moment to gather his scattered thoughts, Ellis slipped his hands behind Cinder's knees and lifted him off the ground.

Yelping first in surprise, then tipping back his head on a howl of laughter, Cinder clutched at Ellis's shoulders. He didn't even try to stop his hips when they discovered the delicious friction Ellis's abs brought to his aching, needy cock and rocked of their own volition.

Ellis's muscles bunched and flexed with seamless, sinewy grace as he carried Cinder from the front door all the way to the master bedroom at the back of the house. Cinder traced his insatiable hands and greedy gaze over every inch of Ellis's body he could reach from the distinctly sexy vantage point of being wrapped around Ellis's torso as he carted Cinder around like he *didn't* weigh one-hundred and seventy-five pounds.

Damn but Ellis was strong and gorgeous and sweet and—

"Oh *god*." Cinder cut off his own thoughts when Ellis dropped them both to the bed, falling on top of Cinder and almost immediately grinding their dicks together. "Yes, more of that, please."

Ellis nuzzled into Cinder's throat, continuing to rock his hips with gentle thrusts that kept Cinder craving more but didn't come near close to enough to give him everything he wanted.

Would anything with Ellis ever be enough? Cinder wasn't sure that would be possible. He'd always want more. *Need* more.

"Can I undress you?" Ellis's soft words feathered over Cinder's neck. "You've done so much to make me feel good, touched me in places and ways I'd never experienced before. I want to do the same for you." He faltered, his breath drawing sharply in before wheezing back out. "I mean, I'm sure others have—"

"No." Cinder shook his head, placing a finger over Ellis's lips before guiding his head up so their gazes could meet. He shook his head again for emphasis. "What we have is different. It's unlike anything I've ever experienced before as well. You've already done that for me. You do it every time you look at me the way you do. Every time you offer me that tentative, loving touch. Every time you let *me* touch *you*."

Ellis nodded, a small smile creeping up his lips. "Well, then, maybe it's time we share another first?"

Tilting his head, Cinder brushed a knuckle down Ellis's cheek. "I want to be all your firsts. Any you have left; I want them to be mine. And vice versa. There's no one else

I want to give any part of me to. Not anymore. Not after you."

Breath hitching, Ellis bit his lower lip. "I…" He blew out on a measured exhale before grinning. "I *definitely* feel the same."

"Okay, good." Cinder beamed to match Ellis before popping his brows a few times in quick succession. "So what's this latest first we get to try together?"

A flare of rosy pink colored Ellis's cheeks, but it stemmed from somewhere lower than usual. His throat blazed with splotchy redness that disappeared beneath the collar of his shirt. "I've never had another man at my mercy." His eyes widened, and he immediately shook his head. "That came out wrong. I don't want to do anything bad, I just… I want to lay you out on the bed, take off all your clothes, and kiss every inch of your skin. I want to touch you and taste you and burn every feel and every flavor into my memory bank. Basically? I want to make you feel good, and I want to be the one doing all the work for once."

If Ellis thought for one moment that doing *any* of those things justified the use of a word like *work*, then he was thoroughly mistaken. Still, Cinder wasn't about to snub the idea of having Ellis's hands and lips all over his body. "What's mine is yours, and that includes my body." He winked and splayed his arms wide. "Do what you will with me, Mr. Tremaine."

And Ellis did exactly that. He took his time undressing Cinder, pressing kisses over each inch of newly visible flesh until Cinder lay fully exposed and trembling. Then, he'd begun the slow, sensuous process of cataloguing Cinder's body with his lips and touch. Just as he'd said he wanted to do.

By the time Ellis finally seemed satisfied, Cinder was a writhing mess of needs and wants unlike anything he'd known before. "See?" he croaked, his fists clutching at the sheets as sweat beaded at his brow. "Another first for us both, because I've *never, ever* been worshiped like that."

"Oh, I'm not done." Ellis's husky voice washed over Cinder, drawing a shiver at the promise it held.

And then… "Ohmy*god*." Cinder's head snapped up at the first touch of a soft, warm tongue against the weeping head of his cock. He watched in mesmerized shock as Ellis traced and teased and touched his dick before finally—*finally*—taking him fully inside the wet heat of his mouth.

Pushing his head back into the mattress, he arched into the feel of his bare cock somewhere it had never been before—inside the mouth of a lover, one who had stayed around long enough for them both to get tested. Granted, they hadn't gone to a clinic yet for the full gamut of tests, but they'd popped by a drug store on the way to Kumiko and Lizbeth's. According to the FDA, the over-the-counter test they'd purchased was about as accurate as a quick results test done by a professional.

Therefore, during the car ride post-surviving Kumiko's drunken debauchery, they'd checked their results and held a brief but decisive discussion. Seeing as how Cinder was on PrEP and hadn't had sex with anyone except Ellis since his last negative test, and Ellis hadn't had sex in *years*—a far longer stretch of abstinence since his own last negative—their results boded well.

Still, Cinder hadn't been sure how soon they'd actually take the condomless plunge.

It was yet another first for them both.

"Fuck, baby. That feels so good." Cinder's voice came out hoarse and high-pitched, but he didn't even care. He'd never felt something quite so divine as the tight heat of Ellis's wet mouth suckling at his most sensitive flesh. "If you don't stop, I'm gonna blow."

For a moment, Ellis's ministrations became more focused, as if he aimed to make exactly that happen. But then he faltered, paused, and finally released Cinder from the heavenly grip of his mouth. When nothing else happened, and Ellis didn't say anything, Cinder forced his eyes open and angled his gaze to meet Ellis's. He grunted, adding a questioning lilt at the end that made him sound so much like Tim the Toolman Taylor that he broke into a brief, frenzied laughter.

Ellis popped a brow and looked at Cinder like he'd lost his damn mind, which only made the incongruous laughter return tenfold.

"Ah, okay then." Ellis chuckled and gave Cinder's thighs a squeeze, followed by offering a lighthearted wink. "Another first. I've never been laughed at while sucking a guy off."

Shaking his head, Cinder pulled Ellis over him until their lips met. Against them, and between soft, butterfly kisses, he murmured, "Not laughing at you. Need you. So bad. You've driven me mad with how bad I *want* right now." Then, he crushed their mouths together, drinking ravenously from the man who had managed to make him feel in ways he never thought possible. Both physically *and* emotionally.

When Ellis, still fully clothed, gathered Cinder against him and buried his face in the crook of Cinder's neck, his muffled words sent Cinder's heart racing. "I wanted to finish you like that, and I will. A million times, if you'll let me. But I... I'm selfish. I also want to feel you inside me. Bare. Just... just us."

Cinder clung to Ellis's shoulders, his sweaty palms clutching at the fabric of Ellis's short-sleeved button-down. How had he gotten so lucky to find a man like Ellis Tremaine?

He never wanted to lose him. He couldn't stand the thought.

"Haven't I made it clear yet?" Cinder threaded his fingers with Ellis's and squeezed. "Anything you want from me is yours. Including *me.*"

Chapter Nineteen

Ellis had sworn to himself that tonight would be all about Henry. From the destination he'd selected for their date, to offering Henry a glimmer of an inkling about how Ellis always felt under Henry's caring, devoted touch.

Instead, Ellis was spread out and naked on the bed in the same position Henry should've remained until he found his release at Ellis's hand. Or, more preferably, his mouth.

Still, it was hard to question the rightness of their current situation when Henry draped his warm, delectable body over Ellis's and pressed their lips together. He moved his hips, slow and languid, causing just enough friction as their cocks rubbed together to make them both moan around their kiss.

When their kiss broke, Henry panted against Ellis's neck, his words coming out in broken, fragmented sentences as his continued movements drove them both to the brink. "I know you have... some misguided belief... that you owe me... an 'all about me'... orgasm... but you don't." He groaned and halted the motion of his hips, ropes of muscle showing in his neck as his jaw clenched and he obviously fought the urge to keep moving.

Sucking in several long, slow, calming breaths, Henry opened his eyes and met Ellis's gaze. "All I want is you. And *us*. While I'll certainly take a BJ anytime you feel the urge to give one"—he winked and popped his brows a few times—"it means more than I can say that you were willing to ask for what you want. And, honestly, babe... Do you think it's a hardship to sink my dick into this beautiful ass?"

When Henry squeezed Ellis's butt to emphasize his point, Ellis laughed and shook his head. "No, I guess not."

"Good, because if you thought for even one single second that making love to you was anything but the *best thing ever*, then we'd have to have words. And right now, I'd really rather chase more physical pursuits."

Again, that playful wink followed Henry's words, and Ellis turned to putty in his hands. Especially when his short-circuiting brain circled back around and repeated said words, getting caught on a single phrase and playing it on loop through his lust-addled, love-starved mind.

No one had ever referred to any sexual act with Ellis as *making love*, including Ellis himself. But with Henry, it felt... right. Ellis groaned and turned his face into Henry's arm, trying to hide the inevitable flush of embarrassed delight heating his cheeks.

"Hey, hey. None of that." Henry drew Ellis's face free of its hiding place until their gazes locked. "Talk to me. Don't bury your feelings. I need to know where your heart is. Did I do something wrong? Say something to make you upset?"

"No, I..." Ellis bit his lip. How was he supposed to tell Henry that his casual use of a common turn of phrase had all but flayed Ellis's heart open? And not in a bad way, but because it made him realize how much he wanted those words to be true. Worse? It made him realize how far he'd already fallen in that direction himself.

Henry remained patient, his warm body still draped comfortably over Ellis despite their focus shifting elsewhere for the moment. Ellis drew strength from his closeness and circled his arms around Henry's waist to keep him from moving. "I'm not good at this stuff. You know, talking about my feelings."

Chuckling, Henry placed a calloused palm against Ellis's cheek and peered into Ellis's eyes with understanding and care warming his hazel depths. "You don't have to be good at it. Just be honest. I don't care if you speak caveman or Gollum or whatever the hell works, as long as you get things off your chest."

"Caveman? Gollum?" Ellis's face cracked into a smile. "What the hell are you on about?"

Henry scrunched his nose—one of Ellis's favorite facial expressions of his because it highlighted his adorable freckles—then grunted a few times and spoke in a deep, purposefully garbled voice, "Me Henry, you Ellis." His face softened into a smile, his voice settling back to his normal timbre. "See? Caveman."

"Isn't that more Tarzan than caveman?" Ellis laughed and shook his head, mentally moving on. "And Gollum?"

Clearing his throat, Henry widened his eyes and darted them back and forth, his lips curling into a maniacal grin. "We hates when Ellises isn't happy. Don't we hates when Ellises isn't happy, my precious? We does, we does hates when Ellises isn't happy!"

"Oh my god." Ellis snorted so loud it hurt his sinuses, but that didn't stop him from busting into ab-cramping laughter as well. "Stop. I can't. No more."

Henry shrugged and replaced the ludicrous Gollum-esque smile with his own cocky grin. "What? You asked, I answered."

"Yeah, yeah." Ellis swiped at his eyes, wiping away tears of mirth before they could slide down his temples.

"How did we go from 'about to bang any second' to 'fits of crying laughter' in less time than it takes to toast bread?"

Switching to a ponderous expression, Henry tapped his chin with a finger as he looked into the distance. "Now, that could be accurate, or it could be a complete falsehood. Depends on if we're talking pasty-as-my-ass white toast that barely gets kissed by the heating element or that dark brown shit my gran used to make me. There was no amount of 'scraping off the burnt bits' that could save that toast. It faced down the fires of Hades before it hit my plate, ya feel me?"

It took Ellis a solid two minutes to compose himself after that, and Henry beamed at him the entire time. Clearly pleased with himself.

"Are you about finished?" Ellis blinked tears from his eyes, no longer bothering to halt their progress as they streaked down his temples.

Henry pursed his lips into a thoughtful pout. "Depends. Are you ready to talk? 'Cause if not, I can go all night—"

"Nope. No. Uh-uh." Ellis rolled his eyes and bucked his hips, surprised to find Henry's dick still rock-hard against his thigh despite their recent rounds of hysterics. Well, to be more precise, *Ellis's* hysterics. Maybe it was easier to maintain a hard-on when you were just *watching* someone lose their ever-lovin' mind rather than experiencing the delirious amusement yourself. "Fine. Okay, I'll talk."

A self-satisfied smirk raised the corner of Henry's lips. "Fantastic."

Despite his chest feeling significantly lighter and less terrified by his own thoughts thanks to Henry's oh-so-perfectly timed comedy routine, Ellis still wasn't sure how to put his reaction to Henry's use of the phrase *making love* into words. That is, until an idea struck, and he grinned. "Well, to put it into the words of a famously talented poet and musician, 'My brain shuts down when you're a heartbeat away, especially when you speak the words I long to hear. Every night, and every day.'"

Henry's lips twitched as he angled his chin to the side. "'Heartbeat Away' lyrics?"

Shrugging, Ellis endured the tingling heat at his cheeks, knowing full well Henry wouldn't let him hide. "It's my favorite song of yours. When it comes up in your set, I always stop everything I'm doing and watch from the catwalk. Even before I knew you were, well, *you*, that song has always..." He shrugged again, his face singeing with endless embarrassment. "It hits me somewhere really deep, you know?"

Henry nodded almost imperceptibly, then dropped his lips to steal a kiss. "Thank you, baby. Thank you for sharing that with me."

Ellis was about to brush it off until he caught the glimmer of tears in Henry's eyes. Instead of downplaying the emotion behind the truth he'd spoken, he pulled Henry back in for another brush of lips. Slowly, languidly, their soft kisses turned heated once more. Their hands sought the feel of skin, and their bodies writhed, seeking friction and gratification after the unexpected break in their search for satiation.

When the moment finally arrived, after Henry had painstakingly prepped Ellis and they were both lubed up and ready to go, Henry rolled onto his back and guided Ellis on top. He encouraged him to take control. To drive them both to the threshold of pleasure and beyond.

And when Ellis did—when their bodies connected in that most intimate of ways, without latex as a barrier—a joint moan filled the room as they grabbed for each other, latching on and refusing to let go.

Even after they found their separate peaks and tumbled off the edge, only a hairsbreadth apart, their hands refused to let go. They held on and rode out their shared pleasure until Ellis's head and heart swirled with the certainty that this was it for him. His heart was owned, inside and out, and he would never love another as fiercely or as fully as he loved Henry.

After they took a lazy shower together, where their hands continued to seek and search and discover and demand, Henry tucked Ellis into bed with a kiss to his forehead. "I'll be right back, okay?"

Nodding, Ellis snuggled into the warmth of the bed and tried to ignore the achy longing in his heart. Even though he knew Henry wouldn't go far, Ellis felt raw and needier than usual. He didn't want to be alone, even for a moment.

But when Henry returned, barely a minute later, Ellis pushed to an elbow and cocked his head in confusion. Henry padded across the bedroom floor with his crooked grin in place, an acoustic guitar clutched in one hand, and a glass jar candle in his other. "Alexa, turn off the bedroom lights."

The room plunged into darkness except for the single soft point of light dancing from the candle Henry placed on his nightstand before crawling into bed. After brushing a hand through Ellis's hair and skimming another kiss over his temple, Henry settled against the headboard with a pillow behind his back and the guitar resting on his lap. "This is Betsy. She's seen me through quite a few different stages of my life and career. We found each other when I was barely a tween, and she's the only acoustic I'll play." He winked. "Wouldn't want to cheat on my best gal, after all."

Ellis lay back against his pillow and smiled as Henry stroked Betsy's sleek wooden neck with the tenderness and devotion of a committed lover. When Henry strummed a few chords and used his ear to tune it to his desired specs, Ellis's heart flooded with emotion.

He wasn't a musician himself, but he understood

how intimate a tuning session was. Especially with a cherished instrument like Betsy. Ellis was honored to be allowed to share this sacred moment between an artist and his treasured tool.

Once Henry seemed satisfied with the pitch of his strings, he drummed his fingers over Betsy's face. "I know it's late, but will you let me play you a song?"

It's not like the question came out of nowhere. Henry had brought his guitar into bed, after all. Yet, for some reason, Ellis's heart bloomed at the thought that Henry wanted to play *him* a song. He hadn't brought it into the room as some after-sex wind-down ritual or to ease himself to sleep. No, he sat there with Betsy in his lap because he wanted to play *Ellis* a song.

"I... Yes." His voice was raspy and breathless, but he didn't bother to put more force behind it when he said, "Of course."

"Good. Then this is for you, Ellis Tremaine." Henry smiled, then closed his eyes as he played the first notes, their crisp splendor filling the room and arrowing straight into Ellis's very being.

They were the first notes of "Heartbeat Away."

Sure enough, Henry's rich tenor joined the ringing warmth of Betsy's strings and carried Ellis's heart well beyond his reach. It was gone forever now. Lost to the beauty of the man seated at his side, strumming an acoustic guitar and singing just for him.

For the briefest of moments, Ellis allowed himself to wonder how Henry's mass of screaming fans would react to a private candlelit rendition of a love ballad sang by none other than the Prince of Pop himself. They'd probably keel over dead, and if they managed to survive the shock, it would be a story they'd tell the world. Every chance they got.

But as Henry opened his eyes and aimed those heavily lashed hazel pools right into Ellis's soul, all other thoughts fled. He allowed the love-laced words to carry him away as Henry's voice wrapped around him like a thick, comforting blanket.

When the song finally came to an end—after more than a few extra repetitions of the chorus that the Colosseum's audience had never been graced with—Ellis floated back to himself slowly. He hadn't even realized Henry had set Betsy aside or blown out the candle until he slid under the covers and used his strong arms to pull Ellis against his chest.

Then, speaking into the darkness, his voice barely above a whisper, Henry murmured, "No matter what happens, I'll never be more than a heartbeat away. For you. Forever."

Chapter Twenty

As Cinder belted out the final note of his first-ever number one hit—a fan favorite he continued to play at every concert as an homage to his roots—the crowd's exuberant shrieks and cheers overtook the theater's audio system, drowning out his delighted laughter. Even after fifteen-plus years of standing on the stage, engulfed by the sights and sounds of fame and good fortune, that rush of pure joy when his fans connected with his music never faded.

The 3D Ballyhoo stage lighting that accompanied the super poppy single still working up the audience came to an abrupt halt, casting the stage into pitch-blackness. If possible, the roar of the crowd grew louder as anticipation heightened the mood.

Cinder used the glow-in-the-dark tape markers to jog offstage without running into any equipment. His band played an instrumental intermission from his latest album while he hustled through a well-choreographed costume change. Two assistants toweled off as much sweat as possible before he tugged a ribbed tank over his head and paused for his makeup artist to reapply eyeliner and powder while his hair stylist lathered on more hairspray and artfully retousled his locks.

In less than forty-five seconds, his disheveled rebel with a side of "chic unique" appearance—Cinder's brand—was refreshed. He snatched his faithful acoustic guitar, and inanimate best friend, Betsy, from his guitar technician before making his way to his next mark.

Despite the stage remaining cloaked in darkness, Cinder's chest swelled as he scanned the house. In preparation for "Heartbeat Away," the sultry romantic ballad they all expected, thanks to the prompt shift in atmosphere, the entire audience had their cell phone flashlights on and swayed in haphazard synchronization. It always made him think of what it might be like to look out the front window of a spaceship going light speed through the stars.

The brief intermission music wrapped up, and a single spotlight beamed straight down on Cinder. Other than the flickering light emanating from the wound-up crowd now hooting and hollering in earnest once more, the deep red glow encompassing Cinder, his guitar, and a wooden stool was the only visible area of focus.

He cocked a hip on the stool and adjusted the strap of his guitar before strumming a single note and grinning when the house exploded in excitement.

Their predictions were true.

Without missing a beat, he slipped into the sweet ballad he'd cowritten with Kumiko as a wedding present for Lizbeth. The only reason it held so much genuine passion and heart was because most of the lyrics were Kumiko's, not his. Most of the songs he had sole writing credit on skirted around the topic of *love* because it wasn't one he was familiar with. Instead, he wrote about friendship and family and any number of other important emotions and events in a person's life.

But recently, that had changed.

He'd known he was teetering dangerously close, so it didn't come as a huge shock when he tripped over the edge and toppled headfirst into love. What *had* surprised him was the catalyst that sent him soaring into the unknown abyss of devotion and fervor and complete, all-encompassing adoration.

It had been that night, about a month ago now, when Ellis took Cinder to Fremont Street in Downtown Las Vegas. Over the course of that evening—their first *real* date and everything that had happened after—Cinder learned what it meant to depend on and venerate the involvement of someone else in aspects of his life he'd always tackled alone.

Ellis had held his hand while he faced down one of his longest held fears and remained supportive while Cinder dealt with his drunk and disorderly best friend. Then they'd gone back to Cinder's, where Ellis had taken him apart, one intimate kiss and gentle touch at a time until Cinder knew, beyond a doubt, he'd been marked for life.

There was no coming back from a love like Ellis Tremaine, inspired without a soupçon of effort on his part.

And tonight, Cinder was going to tell Ellis how he felt.

The audience crooned the final note of "Heartbeat Away" in tandem with Cinder and paused long enough for him to murmur a sincere "*Thank you*," before they broke into another booming reverberation of cheers and shouts and thunderous applause.

Rather than getting off the stool so the stage could be subtly and efficiently remapped for the next song's dance number, he allowed his guitar tech to switch out his acoustic beauty for one of his many electric guitars and remained seated. He held up a hand in a silent request for attention— meant to both calm the fans and to make the horde of technicians running the show, who he hadn't spoken to ahead of time, aware that he was about to throw a wrench into the gears. He also hoped a certain someone watching from the rafters would take a pause rather than returning to his duties.

"For those of you aware of the specifics behind my limited engagement with the Colosseum here in beautiful Las Vegas, you might also know that tonight marks the halfway point of this exclusive arrangement." Cinder waited while the crowd erupted over the knowledge of their fortuitous presence on the halfway anniversary of his Vegas show. He grinned, resting casually over his guitar. "To celebrate this exciting occasion, I've got a special surprise for you tonight."

Again, massive pandemonium broke out, but Cinder motioned for silence and was almost immediately granted his request. "Among other things, I've spent a chunk of my unprecedented free time over these past three months working on new material for an album due to release ahead of my next tour."

Out of the corner of his eye, Cinder caught Kumiko standing offstage left, grinning like a loon. She was in on this little impromptu set changeup and had all but done a literal jig when he'd asked for her help setting it up.

"As a treat, I'm going to share an exclusive sneak peek of a song that holds a very special place in my heart." While the audience worked out their excitement at ear-splitting levels, Cinder turned to face his band and drummed his fingers over the face of his guitar. "Sorry again for this last-minute change of plans, but I can't thank you all enough for hopping on board. Let's do this thing."

Throwing his attention back to the auditorium filled with bouncing cell phones no longer swaying in a recognizable pattern, Cinder blew a kiss to the ceiling. Hopefully, Ellis would catch the silent dedication.

"All right, people. This is 'Until I Found You.' Hope you enjoy."

Strumming the first note, Cinder closed his eyes and let his heart take the reins.

Blessed by success, I'm always surrounded.
Out on the road, I've never felt so alone.
Cursed by fame, I've never been grounded.
All my life, I've dreamt of finding home,
thinking it would be my Neverland.
Until I found you, I didn't understand.

The tales they tell in storybooks
are always so sublime.
There's a happily ever after
for every once upon a time.
But fairy tales never do come true,
at least, not until I found you.

Fleeing what I've known forever,
it was you who gave me shelter.
In your arms I found the answer
to questions I never knew I had.
You taught me how to be the master
of all the things that drove me mad.
But most important, you gave my heart a shove,
because until I found you, I didn't believe in love.

The tales they tell in storybooks
are always so sublime.
There's a happily ever after
for every once upon a time.
But fairy tales never do come true,
at least, not until I found you.

Together, we've written our fairy tale chapter,
a happy story fit for ever after.

The tales they tell in storybooks
are always so sublime.
There's a happily ever after
for every once upon a time.
But fairy tales never do come true,
at least, not until I found you.

As the song ended with a guitar riff solo by Cinder himself, it was met by a silence and stillness he'd never experienced during a live show. His heart, already pounding from the adrenaline rush of performing paired with the emotion brought on by the song he'd written for Ellis, kicked to further life at a dangerous new rhythm.

He cast a glance to Kumiko, who stood agape, eyes wide, and hands raised as if she'd glitched out and froze right before clapping them together. She personified the sense of horrified shock thundering through his veins.

Had he missed the mark that badly? He'd poured his heart and soul into this song, allowing everything he felt for Ellis to bleed into the music without filter.

Then, as if waking from a daze, the audience came to life. They cheered and squealed, their exuberant applause echoing from the rafters. And interspersed among the joyous noise, quiet at first before taking on a life of its own, a chanting began. *"Cinderellis, Cinderellis."*

Heart full to bursting, Cinder stood, brushing an errant tear from the corner of his eye as he opened his arms in gratitude and appreciation. He bowed and thanked his fans with kisses blown to the crowd.

They understood.

Now, the only question was, would Ellis?

As was their habit, they'd planned to meet in the new green room after the show. Cinder always beat Ellis there because Ellis's duties didn't end when the last curtain fell. Thankfully, this evening was one where the theater had planned a meet and greet after the concert, so Cinder passed the time signing autographs and taking selfies with boisterous fans.

By the time security scooted the last of his VIP guests from the room, Cinder vibrated with anticipation laced with a healthy dose of nerves. There was no doubt Ellis would've caught his special performance, as he'd admitted more than once to pausing his work to listen to "Heartbeat Away." Cinder had chosen to premiere "Until I Found You" after that song because he'd known Ellis would be watching.

But had Ellis realized, as the audience had, that Cinder wrote it for him? Had he caught the profession of love wrapped into the lyrics, and if so, how would he react to that knowledge?

When Ellis finally showed up, showered and more pink-cheeked and quiet than usual, Cinder was fairly certain he'd made the connection. But how he felt about it, Cinder couldn't be sure.

"Hey." Ellis rubbed a hand over his nape and peeked at Cinder through the fall of his beachy blond bangs. "That was a, ah, really good show tonight."

Cinder tapered his grin so he wouldn't look like the crazed lovesick fool he was. "Yeah? Any favorite parts?"

Ellis's blush turned crimson, and his gaze fell to the floor. "Ah…"

Not wanting to put Ellis on the spot or make him uncomfortable, Cinder stepped forward and pulled him in for a hug. When Ellis buried his face in Cinder's hair and clung to his shoulders, Cinder's heart melted. "In case it wasn't obvious, that song was inspired by and written for *you*."

Ellis nodded against Cinder's temple and squeezed him tighter.

"There's no pressure to say anything. Knowing I was

able to tell you in my own way, that you hopefully understand those words were meant to say *I love you...* That's
all that matters to me. That you know." Cinder rubbed a
soothing circular pattern over Ellis's back and nuzzled into
his throat. "Because I've fallen head over heels, and every
other cliché you can think of, in love. With you."

Ellis huffed out a shaky breath before pulling away
and meeting Cinder's stare. His pale blue eyes were bright
with a layer of unshed tears. "I wanted to believe, but I..."

Cinder brushed a thumb over Ellis's plump lower lip.
"But you, what?"

Shrugging, Ellis dipped his gaze again. "This whole
thing has been so surreal. I was afraid I'd imagined everything. That you couldn't possibly feel the same way, and I...
I love you too, Henry. So much."

Relief washed over Cinder like a cool winter wave
crashing onto the first sun-warmed sand of spring. He let
the full wattage of his joyous grin spread his cheeks before
crushing his lips over Ellis's. "Those are the prettiest damn
words I've ever heard."

"Nowhere near as beautiful as the words you sang
tonight." Ellis pressed his forehead to Cinder's and rubbed
their noses together. "I almost fell off the catwalk when I
realized what you were saying. What it might mean."

"What it *does* mean." Cinder bucked his hips into
Ellis's, a low rumble working up his throat. "And right at
this moment, it means I'm going to take you home. Then
I'm going to make love to the man who holds my heart as
surely as the sun rises every morning and sets every night."

"God. Yes, please," Ellis whimpered. "And then,
will you sing me our song again? Just for us?"

Cinder beamed, his soul soaring with love and laughter and light. "I'll do anything you ask of me, baby. Say the
word, and the world is yours."

Chapter Twenty-One

Henry and Ellis took turns peeling each other's clothing off, piece by piece. They touched and tasted and teased every inch of newly exposed skin before removing the next article. Gentle and slow and oh-so-very sweet. So many of their sexual encounters had been cloaked in the urgency brought on by novelty, driving them to explore with feverish hands and frenzied lips.

Tonight, it was different.

The lust pulsing through Ellis's system was no less powerful now that they knew each other so well. If anything, that familiarity—paired with the newfound knowledge that their hearts were in sync as well—made the intensity of Ellis's desire rocket off the charts.

Once they'd gotten each other naked, Henry stretched out beside Ellis and pressed his body close. He planted a soft kiss over Ellis's left pec before placing his warm palm over the site. "Every part of your body is gorgeous, but the beauty of your heart surpasses anything I've ever known before. Thank you for sharing it with me."

Tears pricked at Ellis's eyes, and he blinked them away. Leaning on the crutch of humor to keep his overwhelming emotions under control, he cupped Henry's jaw and offered a soft smirk. "Only a Grammy-winning singer-songwriter could still manage to wax poetic even with most of his blood south of the border."

Henry released a whoop of laughter followed by a lewd wink and eyebrow waggle. "What can I say, you inspire every part of my multifaceted *personality.*"

When Henry followed those words by taking Ellis in his fist and offering a perfunctory stroke and squeeze before pulling away with a wicked grin, Ellis all but fell apart at the proverbial seams. Something akin to a growl escaped his throat on the tail end of a whimper before he rolled over and crushed Henry under his larger frame.

Looming over his lover, Ellis narrowed his eyes at the wide-eyed innocence playing across Henry's face. "You know I love a good edging more than the next guy..." Ellis rolled his eyes when Henry's devilish grin indicated he'd caught Ellis's purposeful bastardization of the common phrase. "*More than* the next guy" fit better than *as much as*, considering Henry's penchant for making Ellis squirm—sometimes for hours and much to Ellis's unexpected delight. "*However*, can I put in a request for a timelier reprieve? This once? I have nothing against being the center of your attention, trust me, but I want this to be wholly and completely about *us* tonight."

Henry bit his bottom lip and frowned. "To be clear, I get as much, if not more, out of the time I spend teasing you as you do. *However*"—he mimicked Ellis's overemphasis on the transition—"as always, your every wish is my command."

Rocking his hips so their cocks grazed together, Ellis relished both his own shock of pleasure and Henry's low rumble of satisfaction. He obeyed without question when Henry gave his ass a smack and growled, "Roll over."

After both their test results had come back negative, they'd reverified their commitment to an exclusive physical relationship, which included chucking their condoms out the window. As part of their exploration of each other and of their sexual and intimate boundaries, Henry had suggested Ellis give topping a try. It wasn't anything either of them had ever done—Henry had never bottomed, and Ellis hadn't had the opportunity or desire to top—but it seemed like a reasonable adventure to go on together.

They came away from the awkward and rather comical experience fully settled into their roles. There was no question Ellis was a total bottom, and Henry seemed content with maintaining his top status.

Henry took Ellis's place, covering him with his delicious body and nuzzling into his neck. He threaded their fingers together and lifted Ellis's hands above his head as he nipped, kissed, and licked his way from Ellis's collarbone to his earlobe. "I want you to move in with me."

Ellis froze at those words, his eyes flying open to meet the darkness. They already spent every night together in Henry's bed. Unofficial as it might be, it was the closest Ellis had ever come to living with someone. Hell, Henry was the closest he'd ever come to a lot of different relationship milestones—including being in a relationship at all.

But was moving in together after only a few months rushing things? He didn't want to become a burden to Henry. As things were now, on the rare occasion Henry had other obligations and couldn't see Ellis after a show, Ellis had his own place to go so he wouldn't be in Henry's way. He liked that. He liked knowing Henry could still live his life and their relationship wasn't a shackle around his neck.

Plus, Ellis's current living situation was rent-free. If he moved in with Henry, that would change. Despite knowing Henry would object to both the term and the ideology behind it, Ellis refused to be a kept man. He could make his own way in life and had no desire to freeload off Henry in any way, shape, or form.

He didn't care if his boyfriend made more money than him, nor did he feel emasculated by it, so long as Henry didn't expect him to give up his independence and sense of self as a result of that financial imbalance.

Henry sighed and released Ellis's hands so he could stroke a knuckle down Ellis's jaw. "I didn't mean to kill the mood. I really do want you to move in with me. Not only that, but I want you to come with me on tour when my engagement with the Colosseum is over." When Ellis's chest deflated with a heavy sigh, it was Henry's turn to go rigid. He pushed to an elbow and stared down at Ellis, the moonlight spilling through the blinds reflecting in his eyes. "This isn't some short-term, situational thing for me. I want us to be long-term. If things play out as I hope they will, I want us to be forever. When my time ends here, it doesn't mean *we* end. You know that, right? I refuse to leave you behind. There's no other option than for you to come with me."

Ellis pressed his lips together and scrunched his brow. Was that how Henry saw things? That the only choice was for Ellis to drop everything and follow him on tour? What about his own life here in Vegas? What about his job, his obligations to his stepfamily, the mortgages on his childhood home?

He hadn't allowed himself to think beyond Henry's limited engagement in Las Vegas. A small part of his subconscious was aware Henry would be leaving in a few short months, but he never let that part out to air its grievances. It was easier to focus on the here and now and leave whatever might happen when Henry left for future-Ellis to manage.

Plus, hadn't he just reminded himself of the importance of maintaining his independence with Henry? If he stopped contributing to his own subsistence and let Henry "take care" of him, he would lose respect for himself, and his very existence would become a liability to the continued health and happiness of their relationship.

"It's not that I don't *want* to come with you, but…" Ellis winced when Henry's hopeful expression flattened into an unreadable mask. "I can't leave. I have a job, a family. Obligations."

Henry circled the tip of his tongue along the point of an incisor as he absorbed Ellis's words, then sighed and rolled off Ellis to stare up at the ceiling. Neither of them were in the mood anymore, but Henry's departure still hit Ellis with both a physical and emotional chill. He shivered and tugged at the blankets until they covered his exposed skin, leaving his heart to bear the brunt of Henry's distant silence.

"I want to spend every possible moment with you while you're still here, and am open to trying a long-distance relationship when you go on tour—"

"Long-distance relationships never work. Especially not in my line of work." Henry's voice was eerily flat. Emotionless. Terrifying. "It's not like I can come see you on weekends or anything. The schedule is packed. Days off are spent traveling from one city to another. We might go months or even a year or more without seeing each other in person. That isn't a relationship."

The frigid chill turned arctic, and Ellis pulled the covers tighter around his shoulders, willing their warmth into the frozen tundra overtaking his insides. "We could talk on the phone. Or video chat. It would be better than nothing, wouldn't it?"

Again, Henry was silent for a long stretch before speaking. "For a while, sure, but then…?" He cursed and swung his legs over the side of the bed. After standing, he tugged his boxer briefs over his hips, then stalked across the room to yank the blinds open so the moonlight could spill unhindered into the room, mitigating the darkness.

Turning to face Ellis, Henry crossed his arms over the expanse of his leanly muscled chest and furrowed his brow. "I don't understand why you'd choose staying here over coming with me. I don't buy the job and stepfamily as real excuses. You've said yourself that your heart isn't in this job, and Ray and Suzette are monstrous at best. So what's the real reason?"

Huffing out a sigh, Ellis slid up the bed until he could sit against the headboard. With the blankets pooled in his lap, he was left exposed and vulnerable. "You're right. I don't love being a stagehand when it was only supposed to be a foot-in-the-door position and I can't seem to escape it, even ten years later. Still, it's *my job*. It's how I make a living. It's part of who I am. And as for Ray and Suze?" Ellis lifted a shoulder and fiddled with the edge of the comforter. "Are they perfect? No. But they're still family. And they need me. This is my home. It's all I've ever known. It's all I've ever had."

Latching on to those words, a glint of hope lit Henry's eyes. He sat on the edge of the bed and pulled up a knee so he could face Ellis. "I used to think a home was a physical place, but it isn't. It's a lot more than somewhere you live. It's a feeling. It's warmth and love and every good emotion you can imagine all rolled into one beautiful package."

Henry placed a palm over Ellis's heart and offered a soft, crooked smile. "You're *my* home, baby. You're everything I was looking for during those lonely nights on the road when I thought it was physical permanency I lacked."

Something niggled its way into Ellis's chest and cracked the ice there with a fiery blaze of remorse and guilt and agonizing regret. By refusing to leave Vegas, was he essentially telling Henry he didn't love him?

The temptation was there to cave to the dreadful terror of hurting Henry. To ignore his own desires and concerns. To bend himself to Henry's will. But only disaster could come from such a decision. Just as Ellis feared Henry's resentment if he allowed himself to become a burden on their relationship, so too did he fear his own if he gave up too much of himself to please Henry.

"I love you, Henry. I don't want to lose you, but I can't commit to such a big change when what we have is still so new." Ellis diverted his gaze when Henry's face fell. He couldn't keep watching the pain his words would cause. "I can't leave the life I have here until I've figured out how I can continue being who I am somewhere else. For the time being, this is where I need to be. I need to work, and I need to be here. For Ray and for Suze and for *me*."

When Henry's warm palm cupped Ellis's cheek, guiding his eyes up so their gazes could meet, Ellis's heart pinched. The rejection he'd feared wasn't clouding Henry's eyes. Instead, they swam with tears but spoke of understanding and acceptance. "I love you too, baby. I won't pressure you into doing anything you aren't comfortable doing, and if leaving Vegas to tour with me isn't what's right for you when the time comes, then we'll figure out a way to make it work. Just... Will you do me one favor?"

The tight band around Ellis's chest loosened enough to allow him a small gulp of air. He nodded. "Anything."

Brushing his thumb over Ellis's bottom lip, Henry blinked back his tears and smiled. "Will you think about it? Over the next three months, will you keep an open mind on the subject and see if, maybe, an acceptable middle ground might be found? Something that might give us both what we want?"

"Of course." Ellis captured Henry's wrist and pulled him back into bed. When their bodies were intertwined once more, he brought their lips together for a languid, love-fueled kiss. "If there's an answer, we'll find it."

Chapter Twenty-Two

Cinder strolled through the backstage area, clutching a to-go cup of coffee and grinning to himself. The memory of waking to Ellis's solid warmth at his side wrapped around Cinder like a comforting hug, while the ghost of Ellis's good morning kiss still lingered sweetly on his lips. Never in Cinder's twenty-nine years had he ever been as happy as he was right now.

When he'd asked Ellis to move in and begged him to consider following Cinder on tour, Ellis's initial response had nearly eviscerated Cinder. He'd feared Ellis didn't see their relationship going the same places he did.

But he'd long since laid that anxiety to rest. The past two and a half months had been pure bliss. Even better than the two before that, and lightyears better than his first month in Vegas—the time he now referred to as post-meeting the man of his dreams but pre-realizing it.

Ellis had quietly moved his scarce belongings into Cinder's house the day after their talk, and just like that, they now spent every free moment together without fail.

Although it meant Ellis sacrificing a bit of time out of his day to make the trek to and from Cinder's home, he had claimed it worth the loss of sleep. Especially considering he could often sneak a nap while his security team battled the traffic for him—something Cinder had insisted upon. Cinder might enjoy driving himself now and again, but there was no way in hell he'd let Ellis take public transportation when his security crew had a perfectly good mode of transport Ellis could be safely tucked inside.

Thankfully, Ellis hadn't fought him too hard on that idea. Afterall, if he'd insisted on taking the bus, the security team would've had to as well, and Ellis was nothing if not accommodating to everyone else's comfort and ease.

Still, if Cinder had thought he'd known the meaning of *home* before, there was no doubt he understood now. Living with Ellis was like taking that first breath of life-sustaining oxygen after trying to hold out as long as he could underwater.

He felt like, for the first time ever, he was finally *living*.

The only dark spot left was the wavering uncertainty about what would happen when the final curtain fell on Cinder's Vegas show in only a few short weeks. They'd talked about Ellis coming with him a couple of times since their initial conversation, but Ellis remained hesitant. Cinder liked to believe he was wearing him down, but at the same time, he didn't want to be yet another albatross around Ellis's overburdened shoulders.

If a long-distance relationship was the only feasible route right now, Cinder would make it happen. He'd rework the tour schedule so he had a few longer stretches off every month. And he'd insist Ellis keep living in the desert estate, which would allow him to officially give up the caretaker position. That would mean he'd have days off too.

They could make it work. Honestly, there was no other option. Ellis was the most important thing in Cinder's life. They either found a way around this road bump or they drove straight over it. There was no turning back or giving up.

"Get your grubby paws off me, old man."

Cinder's attention shot toward Lizbeth's angry growl, followed by a ringing smack that sounded distinctly like a palm meeting a well-deserving cheek. He jogged toward the commotion, his hackles already raised. When he rounded the corner and found Lizbeth squared off against the red-faced bulk of none other than Ray fucking Brunswick, Cinder's fury turned venomous.

"What the hell's going on here? Liz, you okay?"

Lizbeth's eyes spat fire when she rounded on Cinder until she realized his arrival wasn't adding to the threat of the situation. "This *prick* is getting handsy and doesn't seem to understand what the word *no* means." She pointed a finger at Ray, who sneered and crossed his arms in a cocky "prove it" move that had Cinder's rage surpassing the boiling point in no time flat.

Fists clenched, he stepped between Lizbeth and Ray. Nothing would satisfy him more than beating this smarmy asshole to a bloody pulp. Considering what he'd done to Ellis after their relationship first became public and several of Ellis's inadvertent admissions about his brutal childhood under Ray's thumb, Cinder had wanted to kick Ray's sorry ass into next Sunday for a long while now.

"I'd suggest you apologize, Brunswick. And make me believe you mean it, or you won't like what happens next."

Ray scoffed and rolled his eyes. "I've got nothin' to be sorry about. The little lady here got things confused, tha's all."

With a snort, Lizbeth stepped around Cinder to glare daggers at Ray. "As if, you creepy bastard. You've been riding the edge of inappropriate since day one. I'm not a wilting flower who's gonna let you get away with blatant sexual harassment."

"It's my word against yours, sweetheart." Chuckling, Ray pressed a fist into the palm of his opposite hand, cracking each knuckle in turn. His glassy eyes shifted from Lizbeth to Cinder and back again. "Poor li'l Lezzy Lizzy doesn't have the best rep with the crew, anyway. Likes to tease and flit around, flaunting that girl-on-girl business. Everyone knows she's askin' for attention, then goes and gets all prim 'n' proper when she gets it."

When Lizbeth reared forward, Cinder threw out an arm to stop her. Between clenched teeth, he hissed, "Go find Kumiko. I've got this."

She placed a protective hand over her belly and turned her eyes on Cinder. "Don't do anything stupid. You've gotta be onstage in less than an hour. No breaking your hand or nose or anything else you need to be your rock star self, 'kay?" She rounded on Ray and smirked. "We can leave the tough love up to my lovely lady *wife*. It's been a while since she's had the opportunity to use her black belt in aikido."

Cinder coughed to hide a laugh when Ray turned ashen and Lizbeth flounced away, her jab hitting exactly where she wanted it to. Anyone who knew anything about aikido would know it was a martial arts style that was peaceful in nature, emphasizing holds instead of strikes while using the opponent's aggression against themselves. It was for self-defense rather than offense, but Cinder wouldn't clarify on Ray's behalf. Let the guy shiver in his boots for a bit.

Once Lizbeth was out of earshot, Ray cracked his knuckles. Again. It was all Cinder could do not to roll his eyes to the heavens and cackle at the boorish show of oh-so-manly strength. Tilting his head and squinting an eye, Cinder gave Ray a slow once-over. "It's a shame it took so long for us to finally meet, Brunswick. And on such *unpleasant* terms."

Ray barked out a coarse laugh. "Don't act all high 'n' mighty with me, boy. Fame doesn't mean shit to me."

"No?" Cinder twisted his face in mock intrigue. "Here I thought it meant an awful lot. You sure got cranky when you found out Ellis and I were dating. I was under the impression it had something to do with who I was. Otherwise, your little temper tantrum over the subject makes even less sense. What is it, then? You don't like to see Ellis happy, or what?"

Face contorting into a mask of loathing disgust, Ray turned away as if he couldn't stand to look at Cinder anymore.

"You'll be gone in a few weeks, then Ellis can get his focus back where it belongs. On work. And his family." Ray made a revolting noise at the back of his throat before spitting at Cinder's feet. "Won't be any more nancy boy shit happenin' once you're outta the picture. I'll set him straight again, don't you worry."

Seething wrath colored Cinder's vision in a kaleidoscope of fiery reds, bruised purples, and pulsing blacks. His muscles vibrated as he fought against the urge to punch Ray square in the nose. Without thinking, he hissed in return, "Yeah? What'll you do if I take Ellis with me when I go?"

Ray's eyes bulged, the muscles in his neck and jaw jumping beneath his mottled skin. "He wouldn't dare."

"Wouldn't dare, what? Live his life?" Cinder's teeth chattered in rage. "Ellis is a grown man who holds no obligation to anyone but himself. If he were to choose to leave Las Vegas behind, along with *your* sorry ass, it would be his prerogative to do so. You'd have no say."

"Wouldn't I?" Ray narrowed his eyes. "We'll see 'bout that."

By the time Kumiko and Lizbeth returned a few minutes later, Ray had taken off and left Cinder seeing angry, exploding stars that tunneled his vision and made his ears buzz and his head spin.

"Where'd that piece of shit go?" Kumiko stomped up beside Cinder and shoved his shoulder to get his attention. "He's *sooo* fired. *Gone.* 'Time to pack his sexual harasser handbag and hit the homophobic highway' kinda gone."

Lizbeth sauntered over and wrapped an arm around Kumiko's waist, resting her head on Kumiko's shoulder with a blissful sigh. "I love when you pull out the protective Mama Bear plus Badass Boss routine. Nothing hotter, I swear."

Cinder shook his head to try and free it of the thought-clouding fury. "Brunswick took off. Probably for the best, because I'm not sure how much longer I was gonna last without punching the fucker's lights out."

Huffing out a breath, Kumiko crossed her arms. "Hopefully, he was smart enough to pack his shit, because I've already called the big man upstairs, and that was the final nail in Raymond Brunswick's coffin. He's been on the way out for a while now, apparently. Too many drunken mishaps and a history of treating staff and talent like shit. I'm glad to be the one to seal the deal. *No one* treats my wife and the mother of my child with *anything* but the respect she deserves."

A wave of guilt washed through Cinder, dampening his anger. He'd known for months that Ray had abused Ellis since childhood. Hell, he had seen solid proof it still went on to this very day. And yet, despite that knowledge, he'd sat back and done nothing to stop it. Then, he'd been nearsighted and selfish enough to egg on the sadistic bastard despite Ellis making it obvious—without even saying a word—that he suffered whenever Ray got pissed.

It didn't matter if Ellis had begged Cinder not to get involved or that he tried to convince Cinder not to worry because it "really wasn't that bad." If Cinder loved Ellis as much as he said he did—which wasn't even a question—then he should've done something a long time ago to protect him.

He should've been the one to get Ray fired. Months ago. And Ellis's security should've been upped and required to monitor him everywhere but inside the safety of Cinder's home.

No, *their* home. That house was only home because Ellis was in it, and no matter whose name was on the deed, it belonged as much to Ellis as it did Cinder.

Resolve pulsing through his veins, Cinder brushed a kiss over both Kumiko's and Lizbeth's cheeks. "Sorry to run, babes. Kumi, give Liz some extra love for me, will ya?"

"I don't need love. I need a punching bag." Lizbeth harrumphed, her arms folded and resting on her oversized stomach.

"That can be arranged." Kumiko gave her wife's shoulder a squeeze before motioning Cinder on. "You go take care of your beau, boo. I've got mine covered."

Tossing them a wink, Cinder headed for the backstage area in search of Ellis. He was done keeping his distance from the man he loved to appease his tyrannical and abusive stepfather. Ray was out, and Cinder and Ellis were going to enjoy the final weeks of his engagement at the Colosseum with no more hidden strings attached.

"Oh, hey, Cin." A flirty giggle followed those words, and Cinder turned to find a vaguely familiar young woman—possibly a teen, undoubtedly an intern—emerging from the shadows. She wore a headset and carried a clipboard, so clearly she was part of the backstage crew. Batting her lashes, she stepped up to place a hand on Cinder's forearm. "Sorry to catch you right before the show. There's a problem with the new lighting cues for 'Until I Found You.' I was going to grab Mrs. Matsura-Hodges, but no one seems to know where she is. Any chance you could give us some guidance?"

Cinder hesitated as he weighed his options. They'd inserted "Until I Found You" into the set weeks ago. To his knowledge, there weren't any recent changes to the lighting scheme, but that wasn't his area of expertise either. Kumiko handled the orchestration of any big changes like that, and she couldn't be found because she was off comforting her wife after Ray's harassment.

There were only two choices. Either he could be a monstrous jerk by blowing the poor intern off so he could go see his boyfriend, or he could be a responsible professional and handle whatever issue was at play and see Ellis after the show as planned.

Sighing, Cinder pulled his lips into his patented grin and performed a half bow at the waist. "I'm at your service, my dear. Lead the way."

The girl's eyes lit up. "Oh, thank you, Cin. I don't know what I'd do without you. You're a true godsend."

When she linked her arm through his and steered him *away* from the control booth, her familiar use of a nickname only his nearest and dearest ever used sparked a months'-old memory. He stopped in his tracks, causing Suzette Brunswick to trip over her feet and come to a much less graceful and rather immediate halt.

"You're Ray's daughter, aren't you?" Cinder narrowed his eyes when Suzette's cheeks flushed. *Guilty as charged.* "Did he send you to distract me or something? What's going on?" A chill of fear lanced up Cinder's spine, and he spun around to stare helplessly toward the rafters. "Where's Ellis? Is he okay?"

"My big dopey stepbrother is fine, don't worry." Suzette smiled with such saccharine sweetness it nearly gave Cinder a toothache. "I don't know what you see in him, Cin. In fact, I think you're barking up the wrong tree entirely." The hand still gripping his elbow slid up to give his bicep a squeeze as her lips fell into an exaggerated pout. "I'm the one you'll make headlines with, not that meathead Ellis. His social anxiety is so bad he can barely string two words together, but me? I was born for the spotlight."

She tossed her long auburn curls over her shoulder and puckered her lips even further. It was all Cinder could do not to laugh. She may be Ray's daughter and could possibly be serving a role in keeping him separated from Ellis for some nefarious reason Cinder would rather not think about at this moment, but she wasn't even legal yet. Nowhere near old enough to be held accountable for her less-than-stellar life decisions.

If Cinder had been expected to carry the mantle of the idiocy that was his late teens and early twenties beyond those years, he'd still be bearing the brunt of his many, many poor choices.

"Listen, doll." Cinder plucked her fingers from his arm one at a time until her hand fell away and her attempt at a sexy pout turned more churlish in nature. "I'm not sure what Ray asked you to do, but I'm not interested. In any of it. Ellis is the love of my life, and I plan to spend every moment from now until the day I die with him by my side. There's no doubt he's the right one for me."

Suzette's jaw dropped, her tiny hands balling into fists that planted firmly at her hips. "If your fans knew what a dickwad you were, you wouldn't *have* any fans."

Shrugging, Cinder backed toward the stage. "Feel free to pass on the word. I don't hide who I am from my fans. They either like me, or they don't."

With that, he turned and left Suzette agape and fuming. As much as he wanted to find Ellis to check on him after her little ruse, his opening act was finishing up their second-to-last song and he still had to hit makeup.

Hopefully, Kumiko would be in her usual place stage left to call the cues by the time he had to go on. She'd send someone to check on Ellis for him. Until then, he'd have to hope Ray hadn't done anything stupider than sending his teeny-bopper daughter to run interference. Because if he'd hurt so much as a hair on Ellis's head or caused even a moment of emotional unrest, Cinder was done sitting on the sidelines.

If Ray hadn't liked the thought of Kumiko using her aikido on him, he wouldn't be a fan of the all-encompassing hellfire that went hand-in-hand with Cinder at his most *involved*.

Chapter Twenty-Three

"Are you sure this is okay?" Ellis's eyes darted around the space, his hands fidgeting with the hem of his T-shirt. "Who's taking over my rigging duties? It isn't safe for—"

"Relax, pumpkin." Lizbeth patted Ellis's cheek before returning to the rhythmic circles she'd been rubbing over her belly for the past ten minutes. "Kumiko has everything under control. They moved one of your crewmates into your role. Nothing has been left dangling. My girl is very, *very* good at what she does."

Ellis nodded and bit his lip when Lizbeth pointed at another of the sliders marked with tape and instructed him to prep for an adjustment at the end of the current song. Without missing a beat, she launched into her next lesson, always two steps ahead of Ellis's spiraling brain.

He had no clue how he'd gotten here. The past hour was a complete blur. Snippets of foggy memory ebbed and flowed into his consciousness. A call coming over his headset from his crew leader, ordering him to the ground. Finding Lizbeth waiting for him with an anxious grin stretching her ruby-red lips. Being tugged toward the sound booth. Standing agape as Lizbeth excused Ray's assistant, who handled the opening act's sound, and beckoned Ellis into the booth beside her.

Finding out Ray had been fired and Lizbeth was in charge for the remainder of Henry's limited engagement. Having to ask Lizbeth to repeat herself—twice—when she told him he was being trained to transfer into an audio engineering role yet to be determined. Asking for a third reiteration when she said there was a chance he might be considered for "a pretty important promotion."

The rest of the show flew by in a similar haze. He followed Lizbeth's instructions by rote, using the knowledge he'd acquired over the course of a lifetime to carry out her demands without hearing a single word she said.

When the curtains closed on Henry's final encore, the house lights hummed to life on their dimmest setting— bright enough to allow for safe movement without blinding the audience, whose eyes were used to the darkness by now.

Lizbeth gave Ellis a tight hug, her baby bump pressing into his back. "You're a natural. I swear. Cin's bragging was definitely justified for once in his life."

Head spinning and ears ringing, Ellis slipped off his headset and stared at the bloodred drape separating the backstage area from the house. He'd never been on this side of the curtain when a show ended, at least not in the Colosseum, and certainly not while standing in the sound booth.

"Does Henry...?" Ellis swallowed and cleared his throat, ducking his head when Lizbeth cocked hers in amused inquiry. "Ah, does Henry know? About this? All of this? About Ray, about... me? Being here?"

Lizbeth pressed a hand to the small of her back and hobbled a few steps until she could sink into her chair. She propped her feet up on the seat meant for Ellis, which his nerves had kept him mostly out of, and threaded her fingers together over her stomach. "Cinder was there to hear the good news about your stepfather, but he ran off—presumably to talk to you—before Kumiko told me I'd been laid out for sacrifice."

Tapping a finger over her pursed lips, Lizbeth shrugged. "He must've remembered he had to get his booty into makeup or something. Either way, Kumiko knows my preggo ass doesn't want the sole responsibility of running this show right now, but she didn't know what else to do. For the short-term emergency, I agreed, but demanded help. We immediately thought of you, got approval from the tippy top of the food chain, and here we are."

So Ellis had *essentially* earned this opportunity for himself. While it was true he only knew Kumiko and Lizbeth through Henry, he'd had the chance to talk shop with Lizbeth and demonstrate a few of his skills during various double date nights over the past few months. He couldn't fathom her volunteering him to be her assistant if she thought him incapable.

And he couldn't wait to tell Henry.

As far as the news about Ray? He hadn't fully processed that yet. What would it mean that Ray no longer worked at the theater? How would that affect... *everything*? His financial situation? His free time? His whole life?

Stretching, Lizbeth reached out a hand for assistance to her feet. Ellis obliged, offering his arm to see her through the thinning crowd to the backstage entrance. He led her straight to Kumiko, who was busy tying up loose ends, then peered around the stage in hopes of spotting Henry still wandering around the vicinity. They were never done at the same time, and he looked forward to spending almost a full evening together.

As Ellis ambled through the busy backstage area, Henry was nowhere to be seen, which meant he was either showering or had VIP guests in the green room. Considering Ellis had no desire whatsoever to get trapped by a throng of Henry's fans, he headed for the room he hadn't slept in for ages but kept as a place to escape during working hours. No sense in giving it up, seeing as how he still served as off-hours caretaker and would more than likely need the place back once Henry left.

The time alone might be beneficial, anyway. Ellis needed to process through everything that had happened before he could even begin to make sense of it enough to talk with Henry.

When Ellis closed the door to his bedroom, shutting out the post-show chaos he was usually enmeshed in, a movement out of the corner of his eye startled him. He fumbled his cell phone to the floor before he'd even unlocked it to text Henry with his location. But the momentary spark of delight when he assumed the unexpected presence might be Henry there to surprise him sank into a nauseating swirl of dread and despair.

"What are you doing here?" Ellis backed against the door when Ray emerged from behind a stack of boxes, his eyes glinting with that unique amalgam of glassy drunkenness and fiery anger that meant certain trouble.

Despite being an inch or so shorter than Ellis, Ray was broader in the shoulders. A few layers of extra padding covered his muscles, but they were there, and they terrified Ellis. Always had. Even when he surpassed Ray in height and his physique gained more strength than his aging step-father's, Ellis remained forever trapped in his traumatized childhood brain whenever he faced Ray. Especially alone.

"You're done early." Ray gripped a half-empty bottle of whiskey by the throat as he stumbled toward Ellis's bed. He fell onto the cot, sending it scraping over the peeling black-and-white checkered linoleum floor. "Suzette says one of the backup riggers was doin' your work. That 'ave anythin' to do with your lil' queer friends gettin' me fired?"

Ellis swallowed and pressed his palms to the door behind him, a reminder to stay present and not let his fear pull him into the past. "I was assisting Lizbeth with the audio, so yeah, I guess you could call it like that."

Ray grunted and tossed back a gulp of whiskey, hissing as it no doubt burned down his throat. He wiped his mouth with the back of his hand and squinted at Ellis. "Quick to take advantage of my downfall, weren't you, boy?"

Squaring his shoulders, Ellis schooled his voice to remain steady. "I had nothing to do with—"

"Like hell you didn't." Ray tsked at the back of his throat and shook his head in theatrical disappointment. "You've been goin' for my job since the day I brought your ungrateful ass on board here."

Ellis had never wanted to steal Ray's job. Sure, he'd wanted to get his foot in the door of the audio engineering career, but he only ever wanted to be Ray's protégé. He wanted to make his stepfather proud of him, not put him out of work. "I never wanted that."

A derisive snort sent Ray into a coughing fit. He downed another long swallow of whiskey once he collected himself. "Doesn't matter. It's done. You'll 'ave to make it up to me. Another couple grand a month should keep me afloat for now."

Another couple of grand a month? Panic flared in Ellis's gut, turning his stomach sour. He already gave Ray most of his income. He didn't *have* another two thousand a month to give, even if he wanted to. His job didn't pay that much.

Scoffing, Ray pointed the mouth of his bottle at Ellis. "Don't worry, boy. You'll get a raise with your *shiny new position*. You can afford to pay your old man a lil' livin' money."

Closing his eyes, Ellis steeled his nerves to take a stand. "I'm sure you can apply for unemployment—"

Ray howled with jeering laughter. "Not when you're fired for cause, boy. Even if the cause *was* made up by a group of bigoted queers with an agenda."

Bigoted queers. Ellis opened his eyes and had to physically stop himself from rolling them. The comedic irony of Ray's choice of adjective reached a new level of ridiculous. "You know, *queer* isn't a slur anymore. The queer community has embraced it as our own again."

Ray stood on wobbly legs and stalked across the room to shove a finger into Ellis's chest. "You're missin' the fuckin' point, *son.* I've told you time and again not to associate with the talent. See what happens when you don't listen? Your little *boyfriend* gets me fired for no good goddamn reason. That's on you. This whole fucked-up mess only happened because you couldn't keep your dick in your pants."

Whiskey fumes spilled from Ray's mouth in tandem with his vile words, and Ellis winced at their joint foulness. "This has nothing to do with my relationship with Henry."

Snarling, Ray grabbed the front of Ellis's shirt with both hands, allowing his whiskey bottle to clatter to the floor. Thankfully, the glass didn't break, but the acrid contents splattered the room. Ellis would be surrounded by that horrible olfactory reminder of this moment for a while to come.

"Do you really think you'll be more'n a blip on that celebrity punk's radar once he leaves Vegas?" Ray sneered and slapped an open palm across Ellis's cheek. "Get your shit together. He's gonna leave you behind and never think about you again."

Anger simmered and bubbled through Ellis's blood, but as usual, the fear outweighed anything else, leaving him frozen to the spot. However, this time, he found the will to riposte, if only verbally. "He can't leave me behind if I go with him when he leaves."

Shoving away, Ray bent to retrieve his booze, barely managing to stumble back upright and to the bed as his faulty equilibrium battled gravity. Taking another swig, he glared at Ellis over the tipped-up bottom of the bottle. "You really think that's how this is gonna go down, boy?"

Ellis couldn't find the strength to respond further, and Ray rumbled out a sour laugh, setting his whiskey on Ellis's cardboard box nightstand. Standing, he returned to face off against Ellis with a sneer in place. "You aren't going anywhere. Your family needs you *here*. Plus, no one else is gonna put up with you like we do. Not for long."

But Ray was wrong. Not only did Henry want Ellis to go with him, but he'd spent the better part of the past two and a half months trying to talk Ellis into doing just that. "You don't know that."

With a snort of laughter, Ray fisted a hand in Ellis's shirt and yanked him free of his door-shaped safe zone. "Actually, I do. Wanna know how?"

When Ellis shook his head, Ray laid another open-palmed smack across Ellis's cheek followed by a backhand that sent him stumbling. Because he attempted to turn away this time, it landed against his left ear, and over his eye and cheekbone. The ringing burn stung all the way into his soul.

"I *know*, because if you even think 'bout leaving your sister and me high and dry, I'll tell everyone who'll listen what he did to her. I'll tell them how he tried to rape poor, underage Suze." Ray's eyes narrowed, and he huffed out a laugh. "No, how he *did* rape her. Your sister's a good little actress, and her loyalties are with *me*. She'll say whatever I tell her to say, and you know it."

Ray's grin turned sinister when the cool rush of blood draining from Ellis's face left him breathless and shaking. "Tha's right. You leave us, and I'll destroy your boyfriend. You think he'll still want you if you're the reason his fans turn on him, callin' him a sexual predator? Of a minor, no less? No matter what happens, that kinda scandal will follow him into the ground. His legacy will be forever tarnished."

"I..." Ellis swallowed, his mind churning with possibilities. Ray would do it. There was no doubt about that. He would lie, and Suzette would back his claim without a second thought. It didn't matter if Henry would still want him or not after that. Ellis would never do anything to put him at risk in the first place, and Ray knew that. "I'm not going anywhere."

With a smug smirk, Ray smoothed Ellis's shirt, then patted his chest. "Didn't think you were. But you know what else you're not gonna do?"

Taking a deliberate step back, so he was out of Ray's reach, Ellis crossed his arms in a self-hug. "I imagine you're going to tell me."

"Tha's right." Ray flopped back onto the cot and scooped up his booze with a wide, satisfied grin. He tipped the bottle in a cheers, downed a swallow, then locked his gaze on Ellis's. "You're gonna end things with Cinder. You want him to leave Vegas with his rep intact, you're gonna end it with him. Now. *Tonight*."

"But—"

"No fuckin' *buts*, boy." Ray leaned an elbow on his knee and squinted a glassy eye at Ellis. "You got a family to support now that you lost me my job. You don't have time to mess 'round."

The cold emptiness of the inevitable spilled over Ellis like a bucket of ice water. He shivered and held himself tighter. If Ellis had to break both their hearts to save Henry's career and reputation, he would. Henry deserved better than a cliché breakup void of a truthful explanation and a chance to have a say in the matter, but Ellis knew Henry wouldn't take Ray's threat seriously if Ellis didn't do it for him. Because if Ray set his mind to doing something, he rarely—if ever—failed.

Chapter Twenty-Four

Trembling with eager anticipation, Cinder paced the length of the green room. After Kumiko had filled him in on Ellis's exciting opportunity to pursue his lifelong dream—made available by the removal of that snake Ray Brunswick, making it doubly delightful—Cinder was champing at the bit to celebrate.

However, despite Lizbeth showing up over an hour ago to kiss him goodbye and take her wife home for the evening, Ellis had yet to surface. Cinder was trying to give him time, assuming he might be dealing with some conflicting emotions surrounding his big break coming at the expense of his stepfather's *much deserved* demise, but sitting around waiting proved more challenging than Cinder had predicted. Especially when he was bubbling over with the need to sing Ellis's praises.

When the door to the green room finally crept open, Cinder whirled around with a big, dopey grin, ready to catch Ellis in his arms. However, one look at Ellis, whose shoulders were slumped and eyes were cast to the floor, had

Cinder's pulse stuttering to a halt. "What's wrong? What happened? Are you okay?"

The door clicked closed before Ellis pressed his back against it, eyes averted. "We need to talk."

What was it about those four little words that could shoot a man straight through the heart? Even when he'd never heard them outside the movies or traumatizing stories told by friends, they still had the power to cut him off at the knees. Cinder sank to the couch like a lead weight had been glued to his ass. "Okay. About what?"

Rubbing the back of his neck, Ellis sighed. "I'm sure you heard about Ray."

Cinder pressed his lips together to halt the colorful curses dancing over the tip of his tongue from making a verbal appearance. "Yes, I did."

If that motherfucker had done something to hurt Ellis... Cinder narrowed his eyes, angling his head as he tried to get a better look at Ellis's face. Assessing for signs of violence.

Clearing his throat, Ellis ducked his head even farther, as if he could sense Cinder's scrutinizing gaze. "Lizbeth offered me the chance to help her since she had to take over Ray's position. I... I said yes, and I..." Ellis tugged at the hem of his T-shirt, rubbing it between his thumb and forefinger. "I need to focus on this right now. I have a chance at making my dreams come true, and I can't... I can't mess that up."

Cinder frowned. "Okay." He drew out the word. What was Ellis getting at? What did that have to do with him? With them? "I fully support that. I was beyond thrilled when I heard the news."

Ellis's eyes drifted closed, the muscles in his jaw jumping as he clenched his teeth. But why? What had him so on edge? Wasn't this a *good* thing?

"I need to... I need to focus." Ellis repeated the empty phrase, still providing Cinder with no hint as to what this conversation was about. Balling his hands into fists, Ellis blurted out, "I can't keep doing this. All of this. *Us*. It's... it's too much. I-I need to focus."

It hit Cinder like a two-ton sack of cement, cutting off his air as it crushed his chest under the painful weight. He placed a hand over his heart, as if he could somehow ward off the emotional blow with a physical defense. "You can't... You don't mean that."

The click of the door opening drew Cinder's watery gaze. He blinked back the burn of tears as Ellis turned away, his hand on the doorknob and one foot already out the door. "I do. I... I do mean it. I'm sorry, Henry. I'm so, so sorry." Voice breaking, Ellis fled. The door slammed closed in his wake, leaving Cinder surrounded by the broken shards of his heart.

By the time he managed to gather the fractured pieces of his world and make his way home—barely aware that Emmitt had to take his keys and stuff him into the passenger side of his own car to get him there—Cinder was in no mood for surprises. All he wanted was to bury himself in the blackness of his room, under the weight of his covers, and not surface until he'd found the will to breathe again. Or not. Whatever.

But the freedom to mope and lose himself to his personal demons was taken away when he trudged into his living room to find Lizbeth and Kumiko lounging on his couch.

Kumiko jumped up at the sound of Cinder's shoes squeaking on the freshly waxed hardwood floor. Her face was pinched as she rounded the couch with her arms open in invitation. "Come here, boo."

Frozen in place, stuck somewhere between spiraling depression and grateful relief that he didn't have to walk into an empty house, Cinder could only stare helplessly at the floor.

When Kumiko's arms wrapped around his middle, followed by Lizbeth's belly bumping into his back as she molded around his waist from behind, the tears Cinder had managed to suppress spilled in earnest. He buried his face in the soft cotton of Kumiko's T-shirt and allowed every sharp arrow of pain and heartbreak to pierce at once, leaving him gutted and ruined, yet buffered from the harshest edges, thanks to his closest friends' warm and soothing presence.

They held him through the worst of his wracking sobs, and then Lizbeth headed off to pour them a nightcap—something alcoholic for Cinder and Kumiko, and something virgin for herself—while Kumiko steered him into the bathroom. She had him splash cool water on his face and rubbed his back in soothing circles. "I'd say I'm sorry for breaking and entering, but I'm not. Plus, you gave us a key. When AJ called and said you were hella upset about something, we came right over. Talk to me, boo. What happened?"

Drying his face with the fluffy towel Kumiko handed him, Cinder sighed and sank to the lip of the large Jacuzzi tub. "Ellis and I... We broke up."

Kumiko joined Cinder on the tub and threaded their fingers together. "Love is never easy, boo. It's even harder when you add fame and money into the mix. Always manages to muddy the waters when both parties aren't on even footing there."

Cinder shook his head. "But it isn't like that with Ellis. It never was. You know I didn't tell him who I was when we first started talking, and once he found out, his biggest concern was keeping a low profile because he didn't *want* everyone to know about us. It's not like he was trying to use me. He loves me for *me*."

Kumiko brushed Cinder's damp bangs from his forehead. "I know he does, boo. But being the partner of someone with the kind of life you live can be challenging on the best days." A smile, both wistful and a bit sad, played over her lips. "I met my first love when she was a rising star, and I was still a nobody running around backstage with a clipboard and a dream. Jillian's level of fame hadn't reached anywhere close to where you're at, and yet, despite my ultimate goal being a career on the road surrounded by illustrious celebrities, I was still overwhelmed by it all. Can you imagine how Ellis must feel, *especially* knowing he never wanted this kind of life?"

"I know, but..." The whiny retort died on Cinder's lips when Kumiko's words sank into his soggy brain. It made sense. Too much sense. Ellis had never wanted a famous boyfriend. He'd tried to keep their relationship secret at first and had wanted nothing more than to live a normal life from the start.

When Cinder hid his identity at the beginning of their relationship, he wasn't just lying to Ellis. He was also preventing him from making an informed decision. Cinder had always—clearly, quite incorrectly—assumed things only went one way. That everyone wanted to be well-known and celebrated. To live a life of opulence and extravagance. Had Ellis ever indicated he wanted *any* of those things?

No. He hadn't. If anything, Ellis had made it as clear as possible that he preferred anonymity to celebrity. He wanted to earn the things he had, not be given them. To live in peace, not luxury.

And here Cinder was, ignoring what Ellis wanted. What he'd tried to tell Cinder he *needed*, time and time again. Instead, far too used to getting everything he yearned for in life without care for what it might mean to those around him to hand it over, Cinder had focused on *his* wishes and desires. He'd begrudgingly given Ellis moments of normalcy, but for all the wrong reasons and paired far too frequently with moments that stretched well beyond Ellis's comfort zone.

For fuck's sake, he'd told Ellis he loved him for the first time via song. And not just any song. He'd chosen to perform a *very* personal love ballad to an audience of over four thousand screaming fans.

Had he been paying attention *at all*?

Kumiko's palm patted Cinder's cheek, drawing him out of his tumultuous reveries. "Don't beat yourself up, boo. All relationships have rough patches, and they're built on compromise not martyrdom. If you really want to make things work, you have to find that happy medium. Give a little, take a little. *Both* of you."

Cinder nodded. Still, he wasn't convinced things were as straightforward as Kumiko made them out to be. Maybe if he'd started things out with that in mind, but was a simple compromise enough to fix the damage he'd caused?

Not likely.

If he wanted to win Ellis back, he'd have to do a lot more than show up with some half-assed negotiation tactic and a prayer. He'd have to come up with something that would prove he understood and wouldn't make the same mistakes again.

He had no clue what that might be, but he would figure it out. Eventually. In the meantime, he would give Ellis the space he'd asked for.

Sighing, Cinder stood and offered Kumiko a hand. "Come on. Let's join Liz for a drink, then you two can wow me with your latest list of baby names."

Kumiko tittered as Cinder guided her back to the living room, where they took Lizbeth's proffered glasses and snuggled on the couch together.

Cinder's heart was still raw and painful, but being surrounded by the love of his found family—one of his truest blessings—helped to ease the ache. He settled between them and allowed their comforting hugs and gentle chatter to soothe his nerves and bolster him for the lonely night ahead.

After Kumiko and Lizbeth eventually returned to their own home later that evening, Cinder wandered around the house, sipping at Kumiko's unfinished vodka cranberry. He replayed memories of the carefree days and nights he'd spent here with Ellis, further solidifying his drive to win back the love of his life.

But when he made his way into the bedroom and crawled into bed alone for the first time in months, the aching weight of despair returned. What little reprieve he'd found from the solace of his best friends' company dissolved, leaving him emotionally bruised and forlorn.

As he curled into himself, pulling Ellis's pillow against his chest as a futile substitute for the warm body he craved, Cinder's hand brushed over something soft and cotton. Considering his sheets were silk, the contrasting texture drew his eyes open as he twisted the fabric around his fingers.

Yanking it free from where it had lodged between the headboard and mattress, Cinder realized it was a T-shirt. One of Ellis's T-shirts. Fresh despair washed over him as Cinder clutched it to his chest, burying his face in the cloth that still smelled so much like Ellis.

As unbidden as the wave of anguish, a strained laugh rolled up Cinder's throat as an absurd realization settled over his shoulders. If Ellis was Cinder's runaway prince—fleeing at the stroke of midnight because he'd only been pretending to fit into Cinder's chaotic world—then maybe this T-shirt was his glass slipper.

Something left behind to give the abandoned prince, moping atop his throne, a bit of inadvertent hope.

Chapter Twenty-Five

66 You're gettin' paint all over the damn doorframe."
Ray smacked the back of Ellis's head and pointed to a
tiny white dot that had escaped Ellis's careful tape job.
"I told you to be fuckin' careful."

Mumbling an apology, Ellis pulled a rag out of his
back pocket and wiped the spot clean before returning to
painting his stepfather's living room. Despite being unem-
ployed, and therefore ramping up the frequency and amount
of his drinking, Ray still found plenty of time to dream up
things to keep Ellis busy.

Which, in the long run, was probably a blessing.

If he hadn't spent every waking moment outside
of his paying job doing whatever random chores Ray had
thought up for him to do that day, Ellis wasn't sure he
would've survived the past few weeks.

After following through with Ray's demand that he
end things with Henry, Ellis had been a mess. And without
the physical outlet his rigging work provided, he doubted
he could've maintained his sanity doing the odd tasks nec-

essary to maintain his room and board at the theater.

It wasn't that he didn't love working with Lizbeth and being trusted enough to be taught and guided by an expert in his dream field—someone he'd come to realize was far better at her job than the man he'd spent a lifetime idolizing. But if his body wasn't beaten into submission when he went to bed each night, sleep eluded him. And without proper rest, concentrating on the intricacies of his audio engineering duties proved far more challenging than surviving a day of mindless physical tasks had ever been.

But that all ended today. Henry's final show was this evening, and after that, Ellis had no clue what to expect. He hadn't heard anything about what would happen once Cinder's crew left and the Colosseum was taken over by the next act. Would he be demoted back to stagehand duties once Lizbeth was gone, or had he been permanently promoted to audio assistant?

Even more prominent was the question of what he'd do once Henry was gone. It was hard seeing him up on that stage every day, singing and dancing and appearing for all the world as if his heart wasn't shattered into a million irreparable pieces like Ellis's. Especially when he belted out the soul-crushing "Until I Found You," with as much heart as he ever had.

Wasn't that what Ellis *wanted*? He wanted Henry to move on. He wanted him to find peace and happiness in a life without Ellis, even though it hurt to watch it happening while he remained heartbroken and inconsolable. Especially knowing he wouldn't have the comfort of Henry's physical presence to dampen the pain after tonight.

"When you're done in here, the foyer needs a coat. Gotta make the place presentable." Ray took a sip of whatever amber-colored poison filled his glass, and leaned against the opposite side of the double doorframe from where Ellis worked. "Our first open house is this weekend."

Ellis froze with the paint roller halfway between the

tray and the wall. "Open house?"

With a snort, Ray downed another swallow. "What'd you think was gonna happen? I lost my job, and you don't make enough to support us both *and* make the house payments. I need money, and there's a decent amount of equity in this old girl."

Pain lanced through Ellis's already damaged heart, and he let the paint roller fall into the tray, heedless of the splatter. "You can't do that. You promised, as long as I kept making the payments, you wouldn't sell the house. *You promised.*"

Ray swirled his glass, the ice clinking against the expensive crystal. His eyes narrowed, but a distant look stole over his face before his frown turned almost sad. "I loved your mother too, and this place has fond memories for us both. But a man's gotta live, and finding work in my field ain't a cakewalk. I'll probably have to leave Vegas to get a new gig, and selling means the freedom to do that. Plus, it gives me and Suze somethin' to live off in the meantime."

Ellis's head swam with Ray's words. They floated in and out of focus until they lost all meaning. He rubbed at his temples in a vain effort at bringing some semblance of coherence to his thoughts. "But... but I broke up with Henry."

Scoffing, Ray narrowed his gaze. "What's that gotta do with me sellin' the house and gettin' outta Dodge?"

It didn't make sense. Ray had made Ellis end things with Henry because... because why, again? Everything felt muddled. The only memory that stood out in stark contrast to the hazy mess swirling around his brain was the very real threat Ray had made. The threat to ruin Henry. To label him a sex offender. To claim he laid his hands—among other things, no doubt—on a minor. Against her will.

But he'd threatened to do that if Ellis didn't take care of him, right? He hadn't wanted Ellis to leave. He hadn't wanted Ellis to stop giving him money or quit doing his bidding.

So if *Ray* was skipping town—if *Ray* was selling the house for cash and fleeing to parts unknown—what did that mean for Ellis? More importantly, what did that mean for Henry? Did the threat still stand, or was Ray wiping his hands of Ellis on all counts, including giving two shits about who he dated?

A cool rush of anxiety blew through Ellis's system before a blast of heated anger took its place. His fingers curled into fists as he rounded on his stepfather. "I've worked myself to the bone so I had enough money to make those payments every month. This was *my mother's* house, not yours. You blew through her life insurance rather than paying off the house like she'd asked, then you gambled yourself into such a deep hole your only options were to take out a second mortgage or lose the house. So I did. Well, *you* did, but I've paid every red cent of it. This is my house far more than it's yours."

Tilting his head, Ray worked his jaw back and forth as he studied Ellis. "What about all those years I paid on the damn thing while I took care of a child who wasn't even mine? Did you factor that into your outlandish claim?"

The hurt tried to surface, followed by the fear, but Ellis wouldn't let them take root. Not this time. "You could've paid off the house *and* paid for my upbringing with my mom's life insurance policy. She made sure of that. It isn't my fault you chose to make poor financial decisions. You were the adult in that situation, not me."

Those final words echoed in Ellis's mind, turning his stomach sour. In all reality, he'd been the adult in his relationship with Ray since far before his eighteenth birthday, yet still, he'd allowed Ray to intimidate and control him.

No more. He was done. Not only was he bigger than Ray, he was also smarter. After peeling off his work gloves, Ellis shoved them into his back pocket and stalked toward Ray. Using his larger size and the seething river of rage running rampant through his system to steel his strength, he pointed a finger into Ray's chest as Ray had done to him countless times in the past.

"I'm done cowing to you." Ellis reveled in the shocked pop of Ray's brows. "You're nothing but a fuckup, and I'm not going to let you continue to bring me down with you."

"You can't—"

"Oh yes, I can." Ellis glanced around the familiar room, but for the first time in longer than he could remember, he really *looked*. Memories of his mother still filled the space. Her favorite rocking chair, where she used to knit while he watched cartoons, was still there, only it had been shoved into the corner and now served as a catchall for discarded clothing items and piles of unopened mail. The bowl she used to fill with rose-scented potpourri sat on the spindly antique end table she'd bought on a whim when she'd taken Ellis on one of their many garage sale adventures, but both the smell of roses and the carefree fun of those Saturday outings had disappeared not long after Ray entered their lives.

He'd claimed to be allergic to "strong scents" and found "thrifting" to be beneath them. After all, he could afford to buy her new things, so why slum around with second-hand purchases?

In reality, Ray had been trying to control Maggie. He'd never liked when she attempted to hold on to something from her pre-Ray years. And that included Ellis.

This house—the place Ellis had struggled to keep for so many fruitless, agonizing years—no longer resembled the home he'd once known. It wasn't his mother's anymore, and the more he thought about it, the more obvious the truth became.

It wasn't the house itself he'd wanted to hold on to. It was her memory. And if being with Henry had taught Ellis nothing else, it had shown him that love didn't require binding to a physical space to be real. After all, he no longer had access to any of the places where he'd made memories with Henry—Henry's home. Henry's dressing room. The remodeled green room, open only to the band and their chosen guests. And yet, Ellis's memories of Henry hadn't faded.

They never would, nor would his memories of his mother. As long as Ellis kept them alive in his heart, it didn't matter where he was. They would always be with him.

A weight lifted free of Ellis's shoulders. "Sell the house. I don't care anymore. In fact, good riddance to you. I hope you find happiness somewhere far, far away. But if you can't, don't even think of crawling back here for a handout."

Seething, Ray glared at Ellis in such a way that, even two minutes ago, would've had Ellis recoiling in fear. Instead, it bolstered Ellis's resolve. He straightened his spine. "Actually, there's one more thing I have to say before I walk out that door and never think about you again."

Ray huffed through his nose and crossed his arms, the liquor sloshing dangerously in his glass. "Yeah? And what's that?"

Drawing up to his full height, Ellis looked down at his stepfather for the first and last time. "That utter bullshit you were threatening to leak to the press about Henry? If you so much as make a peep against him or his good character, you'll rue the day you do."

This time, Ray snorted. "So tough all of a sudden, huh?" He rolled his eyes. "Don't worry. Your little *friend* is safe from me. I ain't got a reason to keep you around anymore, after all. Go 'head and crawl back if you want. Not like it'll last. He's too good for the likes of you."

Ellis shook his head, a mirthless chuckle falling from his lips. "I don't know why I was ever intimidated by you. You're nothing but a weak, frightened old man who's too touched in the head to realize what's good for him and what isn't." He pointed his finger one last time into Ray's face, just to feel the rush of shedding another layer of fear. "When you get wherever you're going, buy a punching bag. Because if it ever gets back to me that you start taking your frail little easily bruised feelings out on Suze the way you've taken them out on me for the past twenty-one years? I'll hunt your ass down and give you a taste of your own damn medicine."

With that, Ellis headed for the front door, then slammed it closed in his wake.

He all but floated his way back to the theater, his fragmented heart finding solace for the first time in weeks. It might be Henry's final night in Vegas, but if Ellis had anything to do with it, there wouldn't be another goodbye in his future.

He'd have to figure out the best way to apologize and fix what he'd broken with Henry, but the love in his heart told him anything was possible.

Especially if he got a little help.

"This is quite possibly the most romantic thing ever." Lizbeth dabbed at her wet eyes with a tissue. "Cinder is going to keel over dead in his tracks when he sees you."

Ellis stood in front of a large three-fold mirror, his arms stretched out at his sides to form a T and his legs spread shoulder-width apart. A willow-thin man with round wireframe glasses and a comb-over bent at his feet, placing pins into the fabric of a pair of steel-gray dress pants.

Standing beside Ellis with a scrutinizing gaze laser-focused on the tailor as he worked on Ellis's slacks, Kumiko hummed her agreement. "That boy's been moping and moaning like someone ran over his dog and kicked him in the crotch all at once. He might short-circuit when all his dreams come true in a single breath."

Rolling his eyes, Ellis tossed a look over his shoulder

at Lizbeth, who had hiccupped out another sob following Kumiko's words. "For someone who claims to be a total badass, you sure do cry a lot."

Lizbeth growled and threw a wadded-up tissue at Ellis's head. He dodged the attack only to be stabbed in the ankle with a pin for his efforts. Yelping, he shot a glance at the tailor, who looked at him with a raised brow, as if to say, "I've told you to remain still. This is what you get for not doing as instructed."

Snickering, Lizbeth held up her hands in innocence when Ellis shot her a glare.

He couldn't believe he'd allowed Lizbeth and Kumiko to talk him into getting a bespoke suit in the first place, but with the deed imminent, excitement bubbled under the surface. Not that he was one to care about his attire, certainly not whether his *expensive-ass suit* was designer and fitted just for him.

But when Kumiko and Lizbeth had taken his cry for help and run with it in this direction, what was he supposed to do? Say no, sorry, he changed his mind?

Wasn't happening. Especially not after Lizbeth had danced in a circle, proclaiming herself and Kumiko as his fairy godmothers ordained to prepare him for the ball with his prince. How was a guy supposed to turn down an exuberantly happy pregnant woman who wanted to dress him in fancy clothes so he could surprise the man he loved and, hopefully, win back his heart in the process?

Henry's final performance had been the night before. After talking to Lizbeth during the show, and meeting with the two of them after it, the trio had made a plan. To celebrate the end of his stint in Vegas, Henry was throwing a fancy dress gala at his gorgeous desert home. It was going to be packed to the gills with celebrities rubbing elbows with the little people who made Henry's show possible, which meant Ellis had been invited.

However, Kumiko and Lizbeth confirmed Henry

didn't think Ellis would show. So Ellis making an appearance—and dressed to the nines, as Lizbeth insisted—would be a definite surprise.

But showing up wasn't enough. Ellis also needed to ask for Henry's forgiveness. Although he still wasn't sure whether he could go on tour with Henry—or whether that was even still an option—Ellis wanted to at least try the long-distance thing. He didn't want to lose Henry forever. He couldn't.

He just hoped Henry felt the same way.

When the tailor finished measuring him and promised to have the expensive rush order ready by the agreed upon time that evening, Ellis followed Lizbeth and Kumiko to a coffee shop down the street where they could strategize further.

With hot, sugar-laden beverages in hand—lattes for Kumiko and Ellis, and cocoa for Lizbeth—they gathered around one of the cutesy metal tables with mismatched wooden chairs. Lizbeth dipped a finger into Kumiko's whipped cream and hummed in appreciation as she popped it into her mouth to lick clean. "Okay, so we've got your sparkly dress in the works. What's next?"

"Sparkly dress?" Ellis squinted an eye. "You better not have sneak-measured me for a sparkly dress, or you're fired and I'm going this alone."

Kumiko snorted and yanked her drink out of Lizbeth's reach before she could dip another finger in and steal more of her whipped topping. "No sparkly dresses, I promise. However, as your fairy godmothers, it is our duty to see you fully prepared to show up to the ball and sweep your prince off his feet."

Huffing in defeat when Kumiko moved her cup even farther out of her reach, and Ellis did the same when her gaze jumped to his, Lizbeth leaned back in her chair. She threaded her fingers over her prominent belly and shifted her eyes between Kumiko and Ellis. "Right, so I repeat, what's next?"

Humming, Kumiko tapped a finger over her pursed lips. "Well, he'll have his suit. And our rental car will be his pumpkin mobile. How about a tiara? Or glass slippers? Maybe a pair of those elegant long gloves?"

Lizbeth covered her mouth with a giggle when Ellis groaned and let his head fall to the table with a heavy thump. She patted his shoulder but continued, humor lacing her words. "I have a better idea. Why don't we ask him *the question*."

Lifting his head to catch Lizbeth pressing her lips together to hide a smile, Ellis glanced at Kumiko and found her nodding at her wife with approval.

With a squeal, Lizbeth turned in her seat and opened her mouth to presumably ask *the question*, but Kumiko held up a hand to stop her. "Wait. Before you say anything, I have to preface this with something important." She pointed at Ellis, her expression more serious than Ellis had ever seen before. "I want it to be clear that what Lizbeth is about to ask you has nothing to do with Cinder, even if it might appear to be at least a *little* about him. Understood?"

"Yeah, this was our decision." Lizbeth placed a hand over Kumiko's forearm. "Cin doesn't even know we're asking you, and no matter what happens between you two, *the question* still stands."

Ellis furrowed his brow. "Ah... Okay."

"Good." Lizbeth grinned, darting her eyes once more to Kumiko's before locking that storm cloud gaze on Ellis. "As you know, I'm going to be a mom soon. As terrifying as that may be." She widened her eyes and placed a protective hand over her stomach. "However, scary or not, I'm in it for the long haul. I want to be a big part of this kid's life, and we don't want her to be raised by a nanny."

Kumiko reached out for her wife's hand, lacing their fingers together and smiling in encouragement.

"Anyway." Lizbeth leaned her head on Kumiko's

shoulder and heaved a happy little sigh. "I've decided to be a stay-at-home mom. Or to be more precise, a follow-my-wife-on-tour mom."

When Lizbeth didn't say anything further, but they both stared at Ellis as if they expected him to say something, he scrunched his nose. "Okay, what am I missing? I mean, I'm happy for you. I really am, but I'm not sure what that has to do with me."

Sending her gaze to the heavens, Lizbeth freed herself from Kumiko's hold so she could lean into Ellis's space, practically nose to nose. "It has everything to do with you. Why do you think I've been training you to run Cinder's sound? I want you to take over as his audio engineer for the tour. Permanently, 'cause remember, I'm gonna be a follow-my-wife-on-tour mom. No more audio engineering for me. Unless, of course, you need a little guidance or decide to, like, break your arm or something. Then I'll be there as backup."

Ellis's brain stuttered to a halt and he froze, mouth agape.

Giggling, Lizbeth settled back into Kumiko's arms. "I'm gonna go with that's a 'yes.' So, slugger, you're gonna have the dress—erm, sorry, *suit*—and now you've got the answer to all your problems too. You can beg for forgiveness *and* promise to follow your man to the ends of the earth while still maintaining your independence. Not only that, but chasing your dreams too. Best of all the possible worlds and then some, if I do say so myself."

"I..." Ellis shook his head, trying to clear the sludge of shock from his inner gears so they'd crank forward and allow his brain to process thoughts again. "You can't. I mean, *I* can't. I've never been an audio assistant. I've never even been a mic wrangler. How can I become a full-blown audio engineer with no experience? That's... That's ridiculous."

Kumiko scoffed. "No, it isn't. My Lizzy is a stubborn creature. She's also very protective of her work and of those she loves. Including Cinder. She wouldn't let just anyone run his audio, and she's impressed with what she's seen these past few weeks. You're a natural. A natural, who, if I must remind you, grew up with an audio engineer as a parental figure. Not a quality stepfather, but he knew his business well enough. And you obviously paid attention. You know a lot more than you give yourself credit for."

"Come on." Lizbeth hobbled out of her chair with Kumiko's help. "We've got a group mani/pedi scheduled in less than twenty minutes. Then we've gotta get you back to our place for a shower and some dolling up. Cinder's hair and makeup manager agreed to swing by this afternoon to give you a trim, so you'll be freshly coiffed to boot."

Dazed, Ellis allowed his fairy godmothers to whisk him away for an afternoon of primping and prepping before the ball. Then, it would be up to him to chase down his prince and secure the happily ever after they both deserved.

Chapter Twenty-Six

Cinder's road crew had spent the day packing up shop and prepping for the tour ahead, which meant they were letting off some much-deserved steam. The shindig was in full swing, and everyone was having a good time. Everyone except him.

It wasn't fair for Cinder to stand under his grumpy little black cloud all night when they'd invited all these people to his home for a party. But no matter how hard he tried, he couldn't find even a marginal amount of joy to lean on as a crutch. Not when this "celebration" marked his last night in Vegas. Not when it all but guaranteed he'd never see Ellis again.

How was he supposed to find happiness and light in a world without the man he loved? Gods knew, he tried. After making a few pathetic and fruitless attempts at reaching out in hopes of talking through Ellis's decision and maybe coming up with that magic compromise Kumiko had alluded to, Cinder focused instead on making peace with the situation.

Clearly, Ellis had made up his mind, and continuing to bang his head against that immobile wall of hope wasn't doing Cinder any good. Still, he hadn't had any better luck accepting it than he had with getting Ellis to talk.

Cinder rubbed a hand over his chest, as if the gesture could somehow dampen the constant ache. He returned a few errant waves from crew members and friends, prizing a smile from his lips in their honor.

He spotted Kumiko and Lizbeth making their way through the throng, pausing to exchange hellos and pleasantries with everyone they passed. Their beaming faces emitted a cheerful radiance only seen with true love in its purest form. When they made it to where Cinder stood, Lizbeth had a glint of mischief in her eyes as Kumiko leaned in to kiss his cheek.

"Hello, boo." Kumiko licked her lips. She was far better at hiding things than her wife, but Cinder had known her too long not to catch the tells she tried to disguise with an exaggerated swoop of bangs.

He narrowed his eyes. "What are you two up to?"

Widening her eyes in mock naïveté, Lizbeth shook her head. "Nothing at all. I can't fathom why you'd ask such a question."

Snorting, Cinder glanced between Lizbeth and Kumiko, both of whom wore a mask of puritanical innocence. "Yeah, you two look as guilty as they come. What have you done?"

Before either could come up with another nonanswer, the DJ's voice boomed through the house. "Ladies, gents, and enbies, I've had a special request that I daresay you're all gonna love. While we don't have a professional recording available yet, please enjoy this live ditty by our host with the most. From an unreleased future album, here's Cinder's 'Until I Found You,' recorded live at the Colosseum."

"What the...?" Cinder scrunched his brow, casting

his eyes across the open-concept living space to where the DJ booth sat tucked into a corner. His stomach clenched and his throat slammed closed.

It couldn't be... could it?

Parting the crowd like the Red Sea, Ellis strolled across the room toward Cinder. He wore what appeared to be a bespoke steel-gray suit with a sky-blue shirt and silver tie. His beachy blond waves were combed back, and his gorgeous eyes shone with the same unshed tears that choked Cinder.

Kumiko gave his arm a squeeze and Lizbeth winked before they stepped aside, allowing Ellis to take over the space in front of Cinder. Under the hushed and mesmerized gaze of the partygoers, Ellis straightened his shoulders and held out a hand. "May I have this dance?"

Speechless, all Cinder could do was nod. He took Ellis's proffered hand and followed him into the heart of the room until the riveted crowd surrounded them, keeping a safe distance, but remaining entranced by the scene.

Ellis pulled Cinder in close, pressing a hand to his lower back and lowering his forehead to Cinder's. "I'm so sorry. Words will never be able to express the level of regret and heartache I feel for the way I ended things. It was wrong for a million different reasons, not least of which is because I knew how badly it would hurt you and I still did it."

Cinder closed his eyes and relished the feel of Ellis in his arms, something he'd been all but convinced would be a gift he'd never know the joy of again. "It's okay—"

"No, it isn't." Ellis shook his head and held Cinder even tighter. "I didn't mean anything I said. I never wanted to lose you, and I never felt overwhelmed. Not where it mattered. Not with us. Not *by* us."

Opening his eyes, Cinder caught Ellis's watery gaze boring into his own, their foreheads still joined close so their words could fall as private whispers for their ears alone. In the background, Cinder's own voice crooned about finding happily ever after, something Cinder had almost given up on over the past few weeks.

Ellis huffed out an irritated sigh and pulled away to glance around the room. His cheeks pinked when he seemed to realize how captivated their audience was, yet he refocused his attention on Cinder. For someone who hated to be the center of attention as much as Ellis did, that gesture alone meant the world.

"I love you, Henry. I was weak and let things influence me that never should've played a role in our relationship. Things that don't deserve to have that much power over me, yet I always seem to... seem to..." Ellis groaned and closed his eyes for the briefest of moments. "I'm sorry. I'm so, so sorry. For everything. I'm nowhere near as good with my words as you are. I mean, I could never do something as beautiful as this"—he indicated the music surrounding them—"even on my best day. I just... I don't..."

Cinder couldn't stop the grin stretching his cheeks or the small chuckle that fell unbidden past his lips. Ellis's bumbling nature had always been a part of him that Cinder treasured, and the effort he made now to get out words that wouldn't come was one of the most endearing and precious things Cinder had ever witnessed.

"It's okay, babe." Cinder stroked a knuckle down Ellis's cheek, planting a chaste kiss at the corner of his lips. "We all do things we regret, and those things are often spurred on by factors we can't control even though we think we should be able to. It's part of being human."

Ellis winced and nodded his agreement. "If it makes you feel *any* better, I finally told those 'things' where they could stuff it."

Cinder drew back his chin and lifted his brows in surprise. "Do you mean...? This was fuckin' Ray's doing, wasn't it?" He took a calming breath when Ellis's pinched face told him all he needed to know. "I'm going to kick that sorry mother—"

"He's leaving town, and he's out of my life. good." Ellis squeezed Cinder's shoulder. "He's selling mom's house. I hate to admit that was the final straw, l it was. When I realized everything I'd been doing, all t. money I'd put into it, that it was all for nothing... That I l. Ray control me and... and I..."

"Wait." Cinder tensed as Ellis's words replayed through his mind. "What do you mean he's selling your mom's house? And what money were you putting into it?"

That hint of pink on Ellis's cheeks warmed to a rosy glow, but he didn't avert his gaze. "I know I was ignorant to believe... Well, anyway. Ray's a gambler. He's run into a lot of financial issues over the years, and when he threat-ened to sell the house I grew up in, the house my mother and I lived in before Ray ever even entered the picture, I panicked. It's... It felt like all I had left of her, even though I know better. So I agreed to take over the mortgage pay-ments if he didn't sell it."

So many things came into crisp, clear focus. How hard Ellis worked to make a living and yet always seemed to barely scrape by. How adamant he was about doing the endless chores and home renovation projects Ray saddled him with, even though he no longer lived under the same roof.

How much Ellis stressed over Ray potentially losing his job.

If Ellis was already paying his stepfather's mortgage, what other threats did he face if Ray no longer had *any* income?

Jesus. Was that why Ellis had ended things between them? They broke up the same night Ray had been fired. Had he gotten to Ellis and made demands on him that made their relationship no longer seem viable in Ellis's eyes? Or worse, had Ray given him an ultimatum of some sort? Something that forced Ellis's hand even though, deep down,

...se Cinder any more than Cinder wanted

For ny ut 'e t

y, baby. We'll fix this. The world doesn't . with us together. United as a team." Cinder .1 Ellis's sweet smile lifted his flushed cheeks. you a favor?"

.ing his head in question, Ellis nodded.

. know this is going to be hard for you to agree to, .1eans a lot to me, so hear me out, okay?"

Again, Ellis nodded, his lips pressing together in ob-
.s apprehension.

"Will you let me buy your mother's home for you?"
.1nder held up a finger when Ellis opened his mouth to retort. "I know you like to earn the things you're given in life,
and I commend you for that level of selfless inner beauty.
But sometimes you have to concede defeat and let others
have the win. Like your boyfriend, for example, who really,
really wants to give you the world and every time you deny
him the opportunity, he gets a little crankier and more de-
fiant."

"I..." Ellis shook his head, his eyes wide in wonder.
"You really don't have to, but... Thank you. Thank you for
understanding me while at the same time knowing when to
tell me to shut up and take your generosity like a man."

Cinder barked out a laugh, overjoyed when Ellis
joined him.

"Plus, I mean..." Ellis's laughing grin turned impish,
and he traced his tongue over his plump bottom lip. "We
can always discuss *compensation* later."

It was hardly the time to be thinking about all the
naughty ways those luscious lips could be put to compen-
satory use, but Cinder's rebellious libido warred with his
better instincts.

"Hey, where'd your brain go?" Ellis had the audac-
ity to look scandalized before breaking into another grin.
"I was referring to *financial* payment, not whatever smut-

ty things were playing through your dirty little mind." He winked, clearly enjoying Cinder's failing attempts at reining in his thoughts. "After all, I've been told, as your newly appointed audio engineer, I'll be making quite a hefty salary—"

"Hold up." Cinder dug his fingers into Ellis's shoulder, his heart rate spiking. "Say what now?"

A playful gleam lit Ellis's eyes. "I said, as your newly appointed audio engineer—"

"Yeah. That. Say that again. I think my ears are playing tricks on me."

Ellis tipped back his head and laughed, twirling Cinder in a circle. "I've been offered a position on your road crew by your tour manager and the incumbent audio engineer, who has decided she wishes to be a road mama instead."

Cinder's heart was full to bursting, sending his pulse racing and heating his skin. "So you're saying...?"

"I'm *saying*, I hope the offer is still open to share your bed and have a few drawers of my own on the tour bus, because I'd really rather not get caught sexting with the boss while sharing lodgings with the road crew." Ellis bit his lip and raised an innocent brow. "But if you're into that kinda thing, we could always roleplay."

"Fuckin' hell." Cinder shook his head, dazed and so enamored he could barely breathe. "I love you, Ellis Tremaine."

Pressing their bodies flush, Ellis smiled. "And I love you, Henry 'Cinder' Cinderford. With all my heart."

As the bridge between the final verse and the closing reprise of the chorus filtered through the room, Cinder trailed a line of whisper-soft kisses over Ellis's jaw until his lips met Ellis's ear. In time with the music playing overhead, he sang the last verse directly to the man he loved. "The tales they tell in storybooks are always so sublime. There's a happily ever after for every once upon a time. But fairy tales never do come true, at least, not until I found you."

Ellis crushed his lips over Cinder's, and the crowd exploded in applause. Chuckling, Ellis nuzzled into Cinder's neck. "In spite of everything, Cinderellis would go on to live happily ever after, after all."

The End

About the Author

Evie Drae (ze/hir/hirs) is a registered nurse by day and a bestselling, award-winning MM romance writer by night. Ze has won first place in seven Romance Writers of America® (RWA®) competitions, including the prestigious title "Best of the Best" in the 2018 Golden Opportunity Contest. Ze was also a double finalist in the 2019 Golden Heart®, in both the Contemporary Romance and Romantic Suspense categories.

One of Evie's favorite things to do is encourage hir fellow writers. To that end, ze started the #writeLGBTQ and #promoLGBTQ hashtags on Twitter to support and promote LGBTQ+ authors and allies while providing a safe space to connect and grow as a community. Ze is married to the love of hir life, is the parent of two wonderful fur babies, and runs almost entirely on coffee and good vibes.

Evie loves to link up with fellow writers and readers. You can reach hir directly at EvieDrae@gmail.com or find hir on hir social media accounts listed below. Twitter is where ze's most active but be sure to check out hir blog too. Ze focuses on reviews for LGBTQ+ authors and allies with the occasional quirky advice/recommendation post just to toss things up.

Website/Blog: https://www.eviedrae.com/
Twitter: https://twitter.com/eviedrae
Goodreads: https://www.goodreads.com/eviedrae
BookBub: https://www.bookbub.com/authors/evie-drae
Facebook: https://www.facebook.com/eviedrae
Instagram: https://www.instagram.com/eviedrae/
Pinterest: https://www.pinterest.com/eviedrae/

Acknowledgments

This book has been a true labor of love, from start to finish. I'd like to extend all the "thank-yous" and send a million hugs, kisses, and chocolate to the following:

First, to Benjamin, the best life partner anyone could ever ask for, who puts my dreams at the top of our to-do list and endures my writing-induced tantrums with grace and civility. To my mother, who instilled the love of reading into me at a very young age. To my father and stepmother, who never fail to ask about and root for my writerly triumphs, and whose support knows no bounds. To my brother Andy, his wife Shaila, and their daughters, Ava and Levi, who will undoubtedly be among my first sales, even though Ava and Levi won't be allowed to read this story until they're at least eighteen. To my whole in-law clan, who love me as if I were a blooded daughter, sister, and aunt. To my Dollface, who always believes in me even when my self-doubt is at its highest. To Becky, who takes the love and devotion of a "twin sister" to a whole new level.

To my endlessly patient and supportive agent, Eva Scalzo, who is always there to hold my hand and respond to my anxiety-riddled emails even though I'm going the indie route right now.

To my senior editor, Desi Chapman, and her amazing editorial staff at Blue Ink Editing, LLC, who helped make my words the best they could be.

To my incredible Twitter #amwriting community—most especially my #writeLGBTQ+ lovelies—who hold me up and keep me going, day in and day out. To Jess, my sister across the ocean, who listens to me gripe and groan and reads all of my books even though penis isn't her thing. And finally, to my alpha reader and BFF, Lily, who holds the distinctive honor of being the first person to ever read my non-academic words. Without her encouragement, love, and late-night pep talks, I wouldn't be here today.

Made in the USA
Monee, IL
03 May 2021

67534023R00132